MELODY ANNE

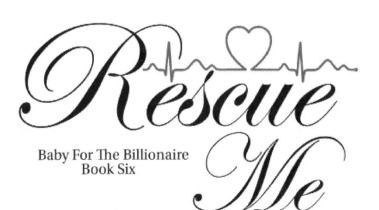

Rescue Me

Baby For The Billionaire
Book Six

Rescue Me
Baby for the Billionaire: Book Six

ISBN-13: 978-1796621877

Cover Art by Adam
Edited by Karen Lawson
Interior Design by Adam

www.melodyanne.com
Email: info@melodyanne.com

 /MelodyAnneAuthor  @AuthMelodyAnne

First Edition
Printed in the USA

OTHER BOOKS BY MELODY ANNE

ROMANCE

Billionaire Bachelors:
*The Billionaire Wins the Game
*The Billionaire's Dance
*The Billionaire Falls
*The Billionaire's Marriage Proposal
*Blackmailing the Billionaire
*Run Away Heiress
*The Billionaire's Final Stand
*Unexpected Treasure
*Hidden Treasure
*Holiday Treasure
*Priceless Treasure
*The Ultimate Treasure

Anderson Billionaires:
*Book One - Finn
*Book Two - Noah
*Book Three - TBD
*Book Four - TBD
*Book Five - TBD

Baby for the Billionaire:
*The Tycoon's Revenge
*The Tycoon's Vacation
*The Tycoon's Proposal
*The Tycoon's Secret
*The Lost Tycoon
*Rescue Me

Surrender:
*Surrender - Book One
*Submit - Book Two
*Seduced - Book Three
*Scorched - Book Four
*Book Five - **Coming Soon**

Torn Series:
*Torn
*Tattered

Taken by a Trillionaire Series:
*Xander (Ruth Cardello)
*Bryan (J.S. Scott)
*Chris (Melody Anne)
*Virgin for the Trillionaire - Book Four - Ruth Cardello
*Virgin for the Prince - Book Five - J.S. Scott
*Virgin to Conquer - Book Six - Melody Anne

7 Brides for 7 Brothers
*Luke: Barbara Freethy
*Gabe: Ruth Cardello
*Hunter: Melody Anne
*Knox: Christie Ridgway
*Max: Lynn Raye Harris
*James: Roxanne St. Clair
*Finn: JoAnn Ross

AUTHOR NOTE

I've been on a health journey now for several years. One day I woke up and looked in the mirror not recognizing myself. I didn't understand how I'd stopped caring so much. It doesn't matter that we're not perfect, but when I was in my early 30s and couldn't walk up a single flight of stairs without breathing hard, I knew I had to make some serious changes.

I spent a couple of years trying to do things on my own. I was a bit more careful about what I ate and I began walking. But I'd quickly lose motivation. It's hard to change your lifestyle when you don't have others around you wanting to do the same.

So I knew I needed help. The next thing I did was hire a personal trainer. I was lucky enough to have found Emmy McCormak on the first try. She not only became a motivating person in my life who helped me lose over a hundred pounds, but she changed everything for me. We can lose weight and still be unhealthy. It's not about a number on the scale. I changed my eating habits, my exercise habits, my routines. I still had setbacks, I still do, but I'm far more conscious of how I treat my body. Emmy has become a wonderful friend who motivates me, pushes me, and makes me believe in myself.

The next step in my journey was to fix things I'd permanently damaged on my body. When you put on over 100 pounds of fat, it isn't kind to your skin. So that's when I met Dr. Movassaghi. Between having children and gaining a ton of weight and then losing it, I had abused the crud out of my stomach the most. I had a tummy tuck surgery with Dr. Movassaghi and I am IN LOVE with the results. It's frustrating when you've lost a bunch of weight and then you look in the mirror and hate what you see. I now like to buy clothes, and it motivates me to work that much harder.

I couldn't have done this alone, I needed people to support me on the journey. I've also made life changes. I love working out, love weight lifting (most days :)), and I have the utmost respect and love for those who've helped me on my journey.

So of course I had to write a hero who is a plastic surgeon, and there was no better way to do that than with Patsy Lander from the Titan family. Some people look at plastic surgery as nothing more than vanity. I might've looked at it that way twenty years ago. But as I get older, I realize we are all beautiful as we are, but there's also nothing wrong with doing something that makes us feel better about ourselves. Plastic surgery also gives people their lives back, such as burn victims, accident victims, and heroes who are injured helping others.

I personally did most of the damage to my body myself. First by having children which left a road map of stretch marks over my stomach. My body didn't like pregnancy :) and then by doubling my weight. So getting this procedure done gave me back confidence in myself and made me want to work even harder than I had before.

At the end of the day all of us have to decide what's best for ourselves. No one can make that decision. And I'm so grateful for people like Emmy and Dr. Movassaghi who are there for those of us who want to do something that makes us feel better about ourselves. I couldn't have done it without either one of them. I also couldn't do it without my friends coming over and pushing me, encouraging me, and making me feel I can do anything.

Thanks for the love and support,

DEDICATION

This is dedicated to Dr. Kiya Movassaghi. You're amazing and I couldn't have completed this journey without you. Thank you so much!

IT WAS TIME for a change.
Dr. Kyle Armistead had what most people would consider a dream life. A world-renowned plastic surgeon, he'd done so many procedures on the elites of the world he couldn't turn on his television without seeing his handiwork. It was something he should be proud of. He was good at what he did.

But instead he felt empty.

It wasn't that he didn't love his job. He'd known from the time he was ten years old this was the line of work he'd pursue. He loved looking at a person as a blank canvas waiting for his magical touch to make it everything they wanted it to be . . . and so much more.

But he was missing something in his life. If only he knew what that was maybe he wouldn't be drifting out to sea without a way to come back to shore.

Maybe it was *because* of his job, but he could no longer see beauty in the world. His life was empty. He'd pulled away from his family years earlier, hardly speaking to them, and then one morning he'd suddenly woken up to realize his friendships were all fake.

It was time to change all of that.

Standing on his back deck, he looked out at the view of the California coastline of endless beaches and bikinis, and knew he was done with it all. It was time to go home. He missed his family. He missed who he used to be.

He had no regrets walking away from this life. None at all. He just wasn't sure what was in store for him next. Maybe he'd find himself again, or maybe he'd discover this was it. He'd never know, though, unless he changed his life.

He'd never know unless he took that first step.

So he did.

CHAPTER ONE

"**E**YORE, GET BACK here!"

There was no way this would end well.

Patsy Lander watched her hundred pound German Shepard take off in a determined sprint as a Frisbee whizzed over the top of their heads. Her normally well-behaved animal must have snuck into the kitten's catnip because he wasn't acting like himself at all.

Taking off as fast as her sandals would allow, Patsy attempted to catch her overgrown puppy . . . but it was hopeless. There was a group of shirtless men with their backs turned to her rapidly approaching dog, and shock and horror kept Patsy from calling out a warning. When she needed to have a voice it seemed to have disappeared.

Though Eeyore was normally calm, loving his naps more than he liked chasing a ball—which was how he'd obtained the name—today he seemed to have forgotten he was lazy. Eeyore leapt into the air as the Frisbee made an arc toward one of the men who was reaching up to catch it.

In horror, Patsy watched her huge dog use the man's beautifully muscled back to launch himself into the air and snag the Frisbee before the man could get his hands on it.

A grunt sounded from the man as he stumbled forward, barely managing to stay on his feet. He did catch himself at the last minute and she watched as his head arched back, watching her dog easily soar overhead to deliver a perfect landing in front of him.

Eeyore, appearing more than proud of himself, sat a few feet in front of the man, the Frisbee in his teeth, his mouth turned up in what appeared to be a satisfied grin. It appeared her very naughty dog wanted to be praised for his impressive catch. Patsy tried to screech to a stop, but her forward momentum apparently was too much for her sandals, and, much to her horror, and the poor fate of the man who hadn't dealt with enough crazy for the day, Patsy stumbled right into his solid back.

He barely moved forward as she bounced off him and flew backward, landing ungracefully hard on the ground, pain instantly flaring in her butt as tears sprang to her eyes.

The man turned sideways, looking incredulously from her to her dog then back to her. Patsy wanted to bury her head in her hands and pray for a freak thunderstorm that would send every single witness of her misery scurrying for shelter. If a few of them were struck, that would be okay, too.

But contrary to most days in Seattle, Washington, the sun remained sunny, and as she looked around the crowded park, she had no doubt she and her dog had gained a *lot* of attention. Finally, Patsy's voice came back and her mouth gaped open as she tried not to stare at the enticing sheen of sweat on the man's muscled chest.

"I'm so sorry. I have no idea what just happened," Patsy said, her voice coming out too high in her rush to apologize.

Just then Eeyore let out a happy bark and trotted over, his prize Frisbee still secured between his teeth. He lay down next to her and gazed at the man, no apology at all in his happy eyes. Apparently he believed the Frisbee was now his.

"Looks like you got shown up by a dog," a guy yelled, laughter coming through loud and clear in his tone.

"Yep. Looks like it," the man replied.

Patsy's stomach clenched at the deep baritone of the stranger's voice. With the adrenaline of the moment dying down, Patsy let her gaze travel up the muscular calves of the man in front of her to the hem of his shorts . . . and higher. What she saw made her mouth go dry as she realized she was checking him out in a very unladylike manner.

Her cheeks heated with color as she shifted her gaze back to the man's worn tennis shoes. At least this was Seattle, and the chances of her running into the man again were pretty much zilch. She only had to get through this awkward moment, then she could be on her merry way.

He dropped to the ground, the muscles in his thighs shifting as his face came into view. Hot damn! Her dang dog would have to climb up the back of one of the sexiest men she'd looked at in a while. And considering she was a plastic surgeon resident, that was saying a lot.

The man was giving her his full attention, and those deep brown eyes seemed to see right into her soul. She couldn't remember the last time someone had looked at her so intensely. It made her already rapidly beating heart practically thump out of her chest.

"Are you okay?" he asked.

Patsy had flashes of a storm returning, but this time she was envisioning the entire park clearing out *except* for the two of them. The instant lust was so shocking she didn't know what to think or say. She'd been in medical school for so long she hadn't had time to sit down and eat, let alone think about men.

But now she was starting a new job and was finally going to feel like an adult instead of a child constantly doing homework. She didn't want, or need, to ogle men. Her career was important to her. Besides that, her brother-in-law, Ryan Titan, seemed to find it his personal life mission to make sure men didn't so much as glance at her. He still thought of her as the child she'd been when he'd married her sister, Nicole, and saved them both.

Patsy would be furious with Ryan if she didn't love him so dang much. But Ryan was the last person she wanted to think about as lustful thoughts toward a stranger in a park filled her mind.

"Did you hit your head?" the man asked, and Patsy realized she hadn't answered him, telling him she was fine.

He reached out and placed his large fingers against her scalp and though there was no thunder, lightning certainly struck as fire shot through her veins. The man's skin was olive, his body solid, and his eyes so dark she thought she could get lost in the abyss . . . and not care to come back.

"I'm fine. I'm sorry," Patsy finally managed to squeak out. She was trying to remind herself she was a sophisticated doctor; she'd been hired by one of the best hospitals in the Northwest, and she didn't need to stay sprawled on the ground like a fool.

"Are you sure?" the man asked, clearly not convinced by her answer.

"Really, I'm fine. My dog has never done that before. I'm so sorry," she said again. She finally managed to rip her gaze from the man's piercing brown eyes to glare at her dog, who looked a bit sleepy as he laid his head down, finally releasing his prized Frisbee. It appeared the game was over, and he was perfectly comfortable taking a nap.

Patsy snapped on his leash to make sure he wasn't planning to run off again, but if he was determined enough, he'd pull it right out of her hands, so she wasn't sure what she would do about it.

"That was an impressive catch," the man told her as he flashed a smile that showed his straight white teeth and made her lick her parched lips. Damn, the man was entirely too good-looking to be released to an unsuspecting public. He should most certainly come with a warning label. "What's his name?"

It took a second for her to realize he was looking at her dog while still grinning. At least it didn't appear as if he was holding a grudge for being used as a launch pad.

"Eeyore," she mumbled.

The man turned and looked at her incredulously before he began laughing, the rich sound better than any music she'd ever heard. She wished she could pull out her phone and record it, just to listen to it over and over again.

Right as she had that thought, Patsy realized she needed to get a hell of a lot more sleep because her brain was most certainly fried to be having such immature and ridiculous thoughts.

"Really? He doesn't seem depressed," the man told her.

"He's normally well-behaved and calm like he is now. I don't know what happened," she said.

As if he knew they were talking about him, Eeyore looked up, his tongue hanging from his mouth as he gazed at the man as if expecting to be petted and told he'd done a good job.

Much to Patsy's surprise the guy leaned down and patted Eeyore's head. "Nice catch, buddy," he said, and Eeyore ate up the attention.

"Don't praise him. He's in trouble," Patsy said.

"We're all good. It's not a big deal, and to be fair, that was one hell of a leap into the air. Let me help you up," the man told her.

He rose to his feet, making those beautiful leg muscles flex and Patsy's mouth water at the same time. There was no way she was reaching for that hand. Her body was already betraying her as it was.

"I'm good," Patsy told him. It took a moment, but she rose to her feet, knowing she would have a giant bruise on her ass, making it difficult to sit for a while. There was no way she was going to show she was in any amount of pain, though. "Let's just pretend none of this happened."

The man's smile widened and Patsy had a feeling he was trying not to laugh at her. His already gorgeous face was even more devastating when crinkles appeared at the corners of his eyes.

"Kind of hard to forget being used as a launch pad," he said with good humor.

"I'm sorry," Patsy mumbled again. She refused to keep looking at him. She needed to get this conversation over with, turn around, and flee as fast as she possibly could.

"No worries," he said.

"I'm late," Patsy told him. She had to get away before she did something foolish like lean in and see if he smelled as good as she thought he might. She tugged on Eeyore's leash and turned around, wanting to run, but forcing herself to walk with dignity.

"Hey!" he called out. "Aren't you going to tell me your name?"

Patsy didn't turn as she raised a hand. "I think we'll leave that a mystery," she hollered as she picked up her pace.

The man didn't chase her down, and she wasn't sure if she was relieved or disappointed. But her heart didn't slow as she made her escape. Luckily her apartment wasn't far from the park, though now she might have to find a new place to walk her misbehaving animal rather than risk running into the mysterious man again.

Or maybe she'd walk the dog ten times a day just to see if she could catch another glimpse of him. She wasn't sure. She decided the best solution would be to call Nicole. She always knew what to do. Tomorrow Patsy started her new job. For now, she could go home and fantasize about a sexy stranger in a park . . . and thunder storms. Today she was still a medical student. Tomorrow she was a resident.

Her life was truly about to begin. She needed to remind herself of that when she had lustful thoughts of strange men. She didn't have time for them. And more importantly she didn't want them.

Sure, her hormones taunted her. Sure, she didn't want a sweaty, sexy man looking at her as if she were his next meal. What woman would desire that? It was a good thing they hadn't exchanged names. Because out of sight could be out of mind.

Settled.

That was most definitely settled.

She was now ready for a new day. She smiled as she told herself she'd never think about the man or the incident again. She was stubborn and determined, and smart. She could do anything she put her mind to. And tomorrow truly would be a brand new day in a brand new life that she couldn't wait to begin.

CHAPTER TWO

PATSY WAS EAGER to start the day as she slipped into the bustling hospital that would be her new home for at least the next four years. This was it. This was what she'd worked so hard for. She was lucky to have a supportive family, a sister who always made her feel as if she was proud of her, and would support her even if she wanted to be a coffee barista. A lot of the people she'd gone to school with after her sister had married Ryan had asked why she'd want to put herself through the torture of medical school when she didn't have to, and Patsy had been disgusted.

For one thing her brother-in-law's wealth had nothing to do with her, though the man had set up a trust fund for her that could support a small country. No amount of arguing had stopped him. She had to admit walking out of medical school without heaps of debt had been nice, but she couldn't help but feel guilty over it.

She hadn't been born to be a socialite just because of who her sister had married. She'd been saved through surgery; it was the beginning of her love of medicine. She'd known from the moment she'd survived she'd do the same for others. She'd become intensely interested in plastics because she loved taking something broken and making it whole again. She'd been given a new heart and though the world couldn't see it, she knew it was there keeping her alive. She wanted to give that same chance to others.

So many people thought plastic surgery was nothing more than a way for vain people to try to hold on to a youth that was long gone. Patsy sometimes thought that way about certain procedures, but she knew there was more to it than that. It wasn't about what was on the outside, even for those type of surgeries, it was about matching how you looked to how you felt, and it wasn't anyone's damn business why someone chose to do something that made them feel better about themselves.

Besides that, she'd witnessed babies having cleft palates fixed and accident victims getting a new lease on life. Plastics was the most satisfying way for her to express herself. Someday she'd be the one in charge, and she wanted to be the best. No, she might not be doing brain surgery or heart transplants, but her work would be seen by the world, and that's why it mattered so much.

Of course today she wouldn't be fixing anyone. That was a good thing. She'd been up most of the night, excited for her career to begin, and not so excitedly consumed by thoughts of the stranger in the park. When she'd finally managed to fall asleep, he'd flashed those dark brown eyes at her, waking her up in a sweat.

Yep, she'd decided she had to find a new park. She couldn't effectively do her job if she didn't get enough sleep, and seeing that man again would surely cause her many more restless nights.

Moving into a large conference room, Patsy didn't bother looking around. It was orientation day and there were a lot of people waiting, eager to begin their new lives.

Taking an open seat, she picked up a packet that was on the table, looking at the impressive line-up of staff with years of experience and prestige behind their names. They could choose to be anywhere, but here they were, preparing the next generation to continue their work.

One of the men began talking, and though Patsy tried listening, his words bored her. It was the typical welcome speech. She should be eating it up, but some people were meant to engage a room, and some weren't. Dr. Watson wasn't known to keep your eyes open.

Trying to stay alert, Patsy scanned the crowd. A couple of people met her eyes and gave her a smile. One doctor winked, infuriating her. It wasn't as if she hadn't dealt with surgeons' egos before. But it still annoyed her that she was often treated like nothing more than a grunt to do their bidding and smile pretty, taking their flirting as a compliment. Her hands might be small, but one day they'd do great things—and she'd earn the respect she deserved, even if she had to beat it out of her colleagues.

Turning away from the guy she wanted to give a crude gesture to, Patsy's eyes instantly stopped scanning as her mouth went dry and her gaze was captured. *No!* She might not have a perfect life, but she was normally blessed with good luck.

As Patsy's gaze scanned the hospital ID clipped to the doctor's coat, and then back to his smiling brown eyes—eyes she was sure to never forget—she wanted to knock herself in the head. How had she missed it the day before? How had she not recognized his face?

Probably because she'd been in shock, she hadn't expected to see the man without his scrubs. Sitting across the table from her was none other than the man who'd kept her awake for too many hours the night before. And he just so happened to be one of the most sought after plastic surgeons in the US, *and* her superior— Dr. Kyle Armistead.

Thankfully, Patsy was sitting, or she more than likely would've fallen on her ass in front of him just as she had the day before. Her stomach twisted, and she wondered why fate had suddenly decided to turn on her. She considered herself a good person, one who didn't normally whine about her life. What did she have to cry about, after all?

Instantly Patsy clung to her bottom lip as she gnawed on it, and since Dr. Armistead's gaze locked with hers, she saw the spark in his eyes as they practically caressed her features and then . . . he winked—just as the other infuriating, and patronizing, doctor had done.

It was a mocking gesture, and they both knew it. She'd refused to give him her name the day before, and now she was in the same room with him; not only did he have her name, but he had power over her career. She'd sworn she wouldn't be one of those stupid students who was attracted to one of her peers, or even worse, to one of her superiors, but did it count when she hadn't known?

She sent him a withering look before turning away, trying to ignore her dry mouth and rapidly beating heart. She needed to get this situation under control. Nothing too terrible had happened the day before. She'd been embarrassed . . . and attracted. There was nothing wrong with either of those emotions. They were professionals and they could move on from this. It was just that easy, she decided, and then her gaze returned to him once more.

It appeared as if his attention hadn't left her. That wasn't helping her frayed nerves—not at all. Realizing other people might be witnessing her internal battle as her face wasn't exactly known to hide emotion, Patsy jerked her gaze away and found a new fascination with the polished table beneath her folder.

She took a moment to analyze the look he'd been giving her, which had appeared to be a cross between amusement and victory. She'd run away, but she hadn't gotten very far. He had nothing to be victorious about. He might have her name now, but that didn't mean he could do anything with it.

With resolve to focus on what Dr. Watson was saying, Patsy chose to ignore Dr. Armistead. She'd been ignoring men for years, so this would be no trouble at all. After two hours in a room that seemed to be shrinking in on her, Patsy wondered if she could develop nerves of steel in this job.

She knew she was making it up in her mind, but it had felt like Dr. Armistead's gaze had been on her the entire time Dr. Watson had spoken and answered questions. It was ridiculous to think that way, but the few times she'd allowed herself to glance his way, he'd met her gaze, his expression unreadable.

This was either going to be a short-lived infatuation with the prestigious doctor, or it was going to be the longest residency ever. Only time would tell which way this would go.

Dr. Watson dismissed the class, and Patsy was one of the first out of the room. Dr. Kyle Armistead was new to the hospital, highly sought after and snagged up as their new head of the plastic surgery department, so he'd be incredibly busy. She could avoid him while still doing her job, while still learning. She made it a goal to avoid him until she could be in the same room with the man without stripping him in her mind.

With that decision made, she felt a lot better. She moved into the changing room and took a deep breath, smiling at the other residents who were eager to begin. She went on autopilot as she introduced herself and chatted with her colleagues.

By the end of her first day, she felt great. She hadn't seen Kyle Armistead since the meeting. It was going to work out. Her luck was back where it was supposed to be—with her winning.

CHAPTER THREE

KYLE WAS A lucky man. He knew it on so many levels that when he didn't appreciate his life, he felt not only foolish but like an ungrateful, spoiled brat. He'd grown up with money, and there had been times in his life he'd rebelled, thinking he was going to make his mark on the world without his family's backing.

What he'd failed to remember was that he was able to choose who he wanted to be *because* he'd been raised by two loving parents and shared his life with three brothers. He was the oldest, and his mother had thrown her hands in the air the day his younger brother Jason had been born.

She'd wanted a girl.

But she appreciated all her boys, making sure they each knew her life wouldn't have been the same without any of them. She'd meant the words.

So Kyle didn't know why it was so difficult to come back home. There were no ill feelings involved, and he didn't have any childhood trauma to confuse the matter. He knew his family had open arms for him. Maybe it was because he felt so lost right now. Maybe it was because he was ungrateful.

He'd only come for two visits in the past ten years, but that hadn't stopped his family from going to him. They made sure to do their visits in the winter when Seattle weather was driving them slightly crazy.

Kyle had to smile as he thought about the last visit with his brother Mitch. He'd decided he was going to learn to surf. That had earned his brother a broken wrist, which hadn't upset him too badly since the lifeguard had then spent the night with him.

Women had always come easy for the Armistead men. Sure their wealth was appealing. Kyle wasn't so stupid to believe it wasn't. But there was more to it than a pocket full of cash. There was confidence money brought that could only be achieved by not worrying about where your next meal would come from or if you'd have a roof over your head.

Kyle needed to be more appreciative of his life.

He smiled as he walked up to a local pub he'd been sneaking into since before he'd turned twenty-one. His long time friend's father owned the place, and it had been a haven for Kyle and his brothers, a safe place they'd come to whenever they came home.

It was a dive in a less than reputable part of town. That only added to the charm of the place. Kyle walked in through the doors, a crowd already filling the tables and bar to near capacity. The seats were scratched and worn, the tables filled with carvings, and the floor scuffed beyond repair . . . and it was heaven.

He looked to the back corner and smiled when he saw Jason sitting at their favorite spot, a cold mug in his hand. His brother glanced up and grinned. Kyle felt ten years of stress fly off his shoulders as he made his way across the crowded room.

"Look who's here," Jason said with a sly grin. "The big bad doctor in a dive bar. Who would've thunk it?" The twinkle in Jason's eyes was exactly the same as when he'd been three, wreaking havoc in the Armistead household.

The four brothers couldn't have been more different from one another. Whether that was by design or an attempt for each of them to show their individuality, Kyle wasn't sure.

Jason was the jokester, always the first to smile in any situation, always quick with his words, and a crowd pleaser. Jason couldn't walk into a room without everyone following him around within an hour's time. He was that guy you just wanted to be with.

"Some of us have jobs we can't run out on," Kyle said as he sat down and looked for a waitress. "You could've had a beer ready for me."

"I did," Jason said. "But you took too long, and I'm drinking it." He didn't look remorseful.

"Mitch and Matthew aren't here, so I can't be that late," Kyle pointed out.

"You know Matthew is up in Alaska," Jason said. "And Mitch did text. He'll be here soon."

Matthew was the smartest brother, hands down. His mind never stopped and his expertise was utilized all over the world. He called Seattle his home base, but in reality he probably only spent a couple months there each year. That made Kyle feel a little better about moving away for ten years.

Mitch was the heart of the family. Well, their mother was the heart, but if there ever was a soul aligned with hers, it was their brother Mitch. He wasn't soft by any means, but he had a heart as big as Texas. He was the one they could count on hands down every time.

Kyle wondered how his brothers would describe him. He was obviously smart as he'd not only made it through medical school but had done so at the top of his class. He knew how to crack a joke, but he wouldn't consider himself a clown. He cared about people, obviously as his chosen career had been medicine. But he couldn't think of any one thing that truly defined him. He wasn't going to ask his brothers what their opinion might be on that particular subject.

"I can't believe you beat me here," Mitch said as the chair next to Kyle pulled out and his six-foot brother plopped down. "That's got to be a first."

"How's it going, Shorty?" Kyle asked with a Cheshire cat grin. Mitch tapped him on the arm with a punch that would've sent most men flying off their chair. It only made Kyle laugh.

Mitch had received the Shorty nickname since he was the smallest of the brothers. That wasn't saying much since he stood six foot and weighed two hundred twenty pounds. Their father was a giant, and each of the boys had inherited his genes.

Mitch flexed just in time for a waitress to appear. She was new, and she was clearly impressed with the man showing off his impressive biceps.

"Well, hello, Sugar. How are you tonight?" Jason asked, and she turned her attention to that brother, looking equally enamored by him. Kyle had to stifle a laugh.

"Um . . . I'm . . . um . . . good," she managed to stutter as her cheeks heated.

"Quit picking on the beautiful lady," Mitch said, and Kyle could practically hear the woman sigh at the compliment. "Can we get another round of beers?"

She stammered a little more before walking off in what appeared to be a daze.

"I can see not much has changed in my absence," Kyle said, finally allowing his laughter to escape.

"Beauty is meant to be appreciated," Jason said.

"I like to meet the new staff," Mitch added.

"I've missed you guys," Kyle said, making the table go silent.

They were definitely close, even when they were apart, but they weren't exactly known for sharing their feelings. Kyle wanted to instantly take the words back as he squirmed in embarrassment.

"It's good to have you home," Mitch said.

"This is getting far too serious," Jason piped in, saving Kyle. "But I do have to agree it's nice to have you here. If we could corner Matthew it would be perfect."

"He'll be home soon and we can hear all about his newest adventures," Mitch said.

"He always has good stories to share with us," Kyle agreed.

The waitress didn't say a word as she left their beers and hurried away.

"I think you scared her off," Mitch said. "And I was hoping to get some food."

"You might be out of luck," Kyle told him.

"I'd just get heartburn anyway. I think they put extra grease on top of the grease here," Jason said.

"But the pain is worth it. I miss bar food," Kyle added.

"Yeah, it's good once in a while," Jason said as he tried to flag down the waitress, who wouldn't look their way.

"How are you liking the new job?" Mitch asked. "It's got to be a real change from having your own practice. Are the boobs as great in Seattle as they are in the land of plastic?"

"There's nothing wrong with cosmetic surgery," Kyle said for what felt like the millionth time since he'd become a surgeon.

"I appreciate plastic," Mitch said with a grin. "I take beauty in all shapes and sizes."

"You make me feel dirty sitting near you," Kyle told him.

That made the brothers laugh again.

"Seriously, how's it going?" Jason asked.

"It's different, but I needed a change. I'm glad I came home," Kyle told them.

He wasn't a hundred percent sure if he was telling the truth or not. He still wasn't sure what he wanted. An image of Patsy flashed through his mind, and he pushed that thought right out the window. He was her boss, and though he'd enjoyed the hell out of flustering her in that meeting, he knew she was hands off. Of course, when had that ever stopped him before? Dammit! She was a challenge he wanted to go after. The fact that she'd refused to give him her name had seriously turned him on. He wasn't used to women running away from him. And that damn dog of hers had made him instantly fall in love. What a terrific animal.

The waitress finally came back and they ordered their pub burgers, fries, onion rings, and cheese sticks. And they polished it all off while catching up.

By the time Kyle left the bar he was feeling a lot better about his decision to come home. He'd meant to talk to his brothers about the mysterious resident he was technically the boss over, but for some reason he'd kept it to himself.

Maybe when he figured out exactly what he planned on doing with the girl, he'd think to ask for some advice. But he doubted it. Kyle had always been a jump-in-with-both-feet kind of guy. Maybe all he needed to do was take the leap now.

CHAPTER FOUR

SOME OF KYLE Armistead's favorite places in any hospital were the surgical viewing rooms. He could close his eyes and listen to the staff on the other side conducting surgery, moving along with them in his mind, asking himself if he'd do it the same way. Sometimes the answer was yes, sometimes no.

But he didn't only love the viewing rooms because of the surgeries taking place. He liked them most during the first month new residents were at a hospital because they tended to not hold back, thinking it was a safe zone. It was a good opportunity to listen, to find out who had what it took to be the best, who would stand out when others fell into the shadows. They never paid attention to him when he sat in the rooms as he normally positioned himself in a corner chair with his head leaned back, his feet up, looking as if he didn't have a care in the world.

A lot of residents would find the viewing rooms a great place to hide away when a surgery wasn't going on. The rooms were dark and quiet and no one bugged you. Whether it was a power nap or a study hour you needed, that was the place to go. On call rooms got too noisy, too smelly, and too crowded.

Kyle had been in this career long enough to know the ins and outs of any hospital. He was good at his job, and he loved what he did. His lips turned up a bit as he tuned out the chatter of the residents.

When a person knows how good they are at their job, they might come off as arrogant. Kyle didn't consider himself a man with a big ego, he just knew he was *that* good. Some were born to yield a scalpel, and others were born to do paperwork. One of the biggest tragedies in life, in Kyle's humble opinion, was when a person didn't appreciate and *use* the talent they'd been given.

It wasn't as if these thoughts went through Kyle's head often. However, as he leaned back in the incredibly uncomfortable viewing room chair, his eyes shut, his mind turned on constant alert, these were the thoughts he was facing.

It was better than thinking about *her*—about his resident who'd been on his mind for an entire week. It had been exactly that long since her dog had used him as a launching pad. He hadn't been able to keep her from his mind the rest of that day, or the rest of the week—especially with her working in the same building as him. It might be a big place, but it grew surprisingly small when a woman was there that he wanted desperately.

After she and her dog had left the park, his brothers had ribbed him endlessly about a woman refusing to give him her name. They'd suggested he should have pulled out the doctor card. He'd been fascinated by it. Kyle honestly couldn't remember a time he'd been interested in a woman who hadn't been flattered by it.

Then luck of all luck, he'd stepped into the room with his new residents and his eyes had been immediately pulled to the back of the room. He'd waited for her to sit down, then he'd sat across from her. He'd gotten to study her for a long while before she'd looked up, before she'd noticed him.

He'd gone from thinking he'd never see her again, to being in a position he'd see her daily, and not only that, but in a position where he was her superior. That meant nothing could happen with her. That meant he'd better never get her alone. He might not be responsible for what happened if that were to occur. He hadn't been this infatuated with a woman in so long he couldn't remember the last time. He liked the feeling way too much.

For an entire week he'd managed to avoid Dr. Lander just to see what it felt like, to see if the infatuation would dim. But it didn't matter that he hadn't been in the same place at the same time as her since he could practically taste her as he walked down the hospital halls. It intrigued him. It also slightly infuriated him. No woman had held that kind of power over him since he was in college. He was sure the appeal would soon wear off. It was just a phase, he assured himself.

Shifting in his seat, he didn't care what the residents crowded into the room were thinking. He heard their hushed whispers, and it nearly made him smile. He'd been in the business long enough to be the best at what he did, but not so long as to forget how it felt to be a wide-eyed resident eager to get his hands on a live patient.

For ten years he'd worked in California, doing surgeries on those who didn't want it spoken about, who liked to slip in the back door and emerge three months later with his perfected face or body and say it was all natural. Kyle had grown bored, so he'd sold his practice, uprooted his entire life and moved back home—back to cold and wet Seattle.

He was happy being home—or he thought he was happy. He could do without so much rain, but the positive was there wasn't a chance of a drought anytime soon. And the spring and summer weather in Washington made the dreary winters almost worth it.

Cracking his eyes open, Kyle scanned the room as residents spoke about their latest conquests, or the money they'd be making when they got through the long hours of training. Kyle had to fight back his annoyance. He was sure he'd sounded just as stupid at their age.

He was about to shut his eyes again when he caught sight of Patsy. She was about as far away from him as she could possibly be in the small room, sitting on the edge of her seat, her full concentration on the surgery going on below as her fingers moved in her lap as if she were down there, performing the delicate cut and stitches being done on the elderly woman who'd been bitten in the face by her neighbor's dog.

The woman's skin was frail and the surgeon who'd initially stitched her up in a crowded ER should've lost his license. The infection that followed that surgery had landed the woman here, where she was now being properly cared for. It was an easy surgery, and Kyle was glad to see Patsy was utterly absorbed, unlike several of the other residents who wanted to see something far more grueling or challenging. It all began with the basics, though. If you could do the fundamentals, you'd learn the rest.

He kept his eyes barely open as he watched her, not wanting her aware he was alert . . . and attentive. It seemed he couldn't really be anything but that way when she was around. It was honestly quite annoying if he dared to admit it.

He now knew exactly who Patsy Lander was. Her sister was married to none other than Ryan Titan, a prestigious and very wealthy businessman residing in Seattle. Their family had money, the kind of money that bought respect, the kind of money that gave people an inflated sense of ego when they hadn't earned it—the kind of money he'd grown up with. That kind of money tended to make the people holding it unbearable in most cases.

Granted, Kyle had to grudgingly admit he liked the Titan family. His family had known theirs for a very long time, and they weren't the typical elitists. However, that didn't mean Patsy was the same. For all Kyle knew being a surgeon was nothing more to her than *playing* doctor because she was bored.

As he watched her intense concentration he realized he was wrong about that. A person didn't make it through that much schooling without truly wanting to be a doctor. That didn't mean the person would be any good at their job, but normally within an hour of meeting a resident Kyle could tell if they had what it took. He didn't want to admit it out loud, but Patsy definitely had it.

He wanted to see her as a spoiled heiress with more concern over her thousand dollar heels than her patients, but he didn't see that. It also wasn't as if he could throw stones or anything. Wealth had been an easy part of his life for so long he wouldn't know what it was like to go without. If he didn't want to work again, he didn't have to. He'd sold his practice and decided to go to a teaching hospital—not because he needed to, but because he couldn't quit doing what he loved, he couldn't help wanting to be known for more than just boobs and asses.

A surgeon could never quit being a doctor. It was in their blood. If he didn't get to cut, he wouldn't survive. It defined who he was, what he wanted, and his purpose in life. The moment he put on scrubs, he knew what to do. There hadn't been a puzzle yet he hadn't been able to solve, and he'd sought out cases other surgeons refused to do. Those cases had been in the beginning before he'd moved to California. Once there, he'd wanted to be sought after, wanted to be the best.

He'd slowly lost himself as he'd gained a reputation for being the best at what he did. Now he was hoping to be remembered in an entirely different way. He was getting back to his roots, to the beginning, when fixing someone changed that person's life. He had no doubt he'd do exactly that.

Yeah, Kyle was arrogant, but it was born of ability. He could perform procedures others couldn't, and that gave a person the confidence to walk with their head held high. Even with all that knowledge, Kyle's thoughts kept returning to Patsy, and he was beginning to grow irritated with her because of it. Logically he knew it wasn't her fault. She wasn't flirting with him, wasn't doing all those things a lot of women did in his presence to gain his attention, but maybe she was a lot more subtle about it. He couldn't imagine her not being affected by the chemistry between them. That was something that didn't happen every day.

One of the residents got a little excited behind him and kicked his chair, making a low rumble of disapproval escape Kyle's throat. The residents grew amusingly silent. There was something to be said about inspiring fear in the new generation. Respect quickly followed.

As much as Kyle had enjoyed running his own show for ten years, it was nice to be back in the hustle and bustle of a busy hospital. As much as this younger generation annoyed him at times, he also thrived on their eagerness to learn, their excitement over procedures that had long ago bored him. There was something to be said about going back to the basics.

Still only half watching the surgery below, Kyle was far more interested in what Patsy was doing. He wasn't sure if she was aware he was there or not, but he found it hard to believe anyone could ignore his presence. She was sitting up too properly, making sure her head was turned just so, and even when the group behind him got a little too loud, she didn't so much as turn an inch to check it out.

The surgery wasn't all that interesting so he had a feeling she was more than aware of him sitting nearby, and she was doing her damnedest to pretend he didn't exist. That was okay with him. It was probably better for both of them if they kept it that way. The last thing he needed was to have an affair with not only someone he was responsible for, but a spoiled little heiress at that. Girls like her required far too much work, and he couldn't simply disappear in the morning.

Yeah, he was an ass. Get over it.

Kyle was so aware of Patsy's movements, it made him smile when she rose and practically hugged the window in front of her as she began making her way past him. There was no other way around if she wanted to leave the room.

He thought about being an ass and stretching his legs out far in front of him so she'd have to climb over him, but that might be pushing this silent game a little too far. He did notice she glanced at him out of the corner of her eye before ripping her gaze away again. Interesting. It appeared as if everything she did kept him entertained.

"Okay kids, whoever gets here first can close up," Dr. Watson called over the speaker in the room.

Oh Crap!

There was utter silence before the room erupted as the residents rushed from their seats, pushing each other out of the way as if they were no older than a group of elementary school kids.

As a group of residents pushed past the two of them, Patsy turned and looked at him, her eyes widening when she noticed his own were open and gazing directly at her. That color she couldn't seem to manage to keep from her cheeks instantly lit up her beautiful face, making him want to reach out for her.

Dang it, he couldn't seem to resist the innocence a blush spoke on a woman's cheeks. How could she still have enough of it left to color her face? Maybe it was an act. If it was, she was damn good.

"This one's mine," one of the residents yelled as he pushed past Patsy, knocking her off her feet. Kyle watched as she began to topple, knowing this wasn't going to end well. It seemed the pretty doctor might be slightly klutzy—just one more thing that was endearing about her.

Before Kyle thought of reaching for her, Patsy went flying—straight on top of him. And though she was a small thing, though her curves were ample enough for him to fantasize about filling his hands with, she landed hard right in the middle of his lap.

Their cries mingled together, hers of shock, his of pain as she squished a part of him he'd much rather keep protected. It took him a second to clear the flashing lights popping in front of his eyes and another second to realize he had an amazingly great smelling, perfectly curvy, beautiful woman wiggling in his lap.

Though he knew she was struggling to untwist herself and rise to her feet, the resident who'd knocked her over wasn't the last to shuffle from the room, and they weren't even noticed as people climbed over them, making Patsy wiggle on top of him, giving him a reaction there was no way he was going to be able to hide from her.

As all the blood rushed to one sensitive area of his body, Kyle's arms wrapped around Patsy to keep her from wiggling. His body was now pulsing, his blood on fire. Her face was too close to his and the single most important thought in his head was how good her lips would taste.

It had been way too long since he'd spent the night with a woman, and now he'd literally had one land right in his lap and his body had ideas his brain knew would be the wrong path to take.

Kyle didn't try to stop the groan of pleasure from slipping from his throat as the rest of the room cleared, leaving them alone. He could take her right here on this chair and no one would be the wiser. The other residents were long gone. His head shifted forward without his brain allowing him to stop it.

Patsy instantly put a stop to it as she held a hand against his chest, her eyes wide, her breathing heavy as her gaze focused on his lips. He was pretty sure her brain and body were having the same battle as his.

Kyle wasn't sure how much more torture he could take, but finally he shifted her, slowly turning her body, groaning again as she did a half turn on his throbbing lap. Then he pushed her to her feet, his hands staying on her luscious hips a few seconds longer than necessary. He seriously wouldn't mind placing them there without any clothes in the way.

The flush in her cheeks deepened as he refused to release her gaze. She must've been as mesmerized as he was because she wasn't struggling against his hold as she stood with what appeared to be shaky knees.

There was certainly something going on between the two of them—whether they wanted there to be or not. Kyle wasn't too sure he was going to continue to be able to stop this. He knew he should—but he wasn't sure how much longer he was going to be able to think with the smarter of his brains.

"It appears as if you like falling for me," Kyle finally said, forcing a crooked smile to his lips.

There might not be a way to hide his body's reaction at having her sweet ass rub on his lap, but there was no way he wanted her to know how desperately he wanted her. Most men would get hard with those curves pressed against them. But Kyle knew there was more to his desire than an ass against his groin. No. There was something about this woman that was refusing him relief.

"I'm sorry. I should've been more careful," she said, her voice husky, making his body more rigid than it had been a moment before. Damn, he wanted to get her to a bedroom—or any horizontal place. He had to remind himself what a bad idea that would be.

"This one wasn't your fault," he told her, forcing his grin to grow cockier. Maybe it would be better to irritate her so she'd stomp off. If not he feared he'd pull her back onto his lap and see who could get their clothes off the fastest.

"Technically the other one wasn't my fault either," she told him as she took a step away. "It was Eeyore's." She regained her composure. Interesting how she protected herself. He wondered what her story was.

She reached up and ran a hand down the center of her chest, instantly drawing his gaze to her breasts. They'd been pressed against him, and he had no doubt they were all natural. He definitely wanted to see for himself. He had to push that thought out of his mind.

Seeing where his gaze had gone, her eyes narrowed as she quickly dropped her hand and took another step away. Her cheeks were flushed, but while his body was as hard as ever, she was pulling herself together. It was normally the reverse when he was with the opposite sex. He liked to leave them wanting more.

"It's not good to blame things on other people . . . or dogs," he told her with a chuckle.

She rolled her eyes and for some reason that was a challenge. He stood up and took a deliberate step in her direction that made the newfound confidence drain from her eyes as she retreated.

It had been a while since he'd felt the need to chase a woman, and right now he felt like a hunter cornering his prey. Of course, this hunt would end in ultimate pleasure for all parties involved.

"Stop," she said, holding up her hand before dropping it again as if she was afraid to come into contact with any part of him. That was probably a wise decision; he already felt as if he was about to go up in flames at any second.

"I'm not sure what's going on here," he told her. He did stop, but it took the ultimate willpower on his part to do so. This was all so foreign to him, he didn't know what to think about it.

He allowed his gaze to cascade over her body, taking in her youthful face, full lips, slender neck, and flared hips. She was utter perfection, didn't need a single thing changed on her entire body—a masterpiece many women would pay hundreds of thousands of dollars to achieve.

"Absolutely *nothing* is going on," Patsy told him. Her voice was husky again, but she took in a deep breath, turned, and began walking away.

Kyle had the desperate need to chase her down, pin her to the wall, and prove to her there indeed *was* something happening between them. But he knew if he did that, the two of them were going to do something they might regret.

Though as soon as he had that thought, he knew it was false. There was no way he'd regret doing anything with Patsy. But on the other hand he wasn't looking for a relationship, and one-night stands tended to get messy when it came to people you worked with.

It looked as if he'd be dealing with a throbbing body the rest of the shift and probably long into the night. Damn her, and damn him. Maybe the two of them could take a trip to hell together. That might be where this would end up.

CHAPTER FIVE

PATSY WAS DOWN two halls and an entire floor before she felt air returning to her lungs in a proper way. It was a good thing she was in a hospital because she wasn't sure what in the hell was going on with her body—possibly a heart attack. Maybe even a complete body shutdown, or just losing her mind. She could go to the dang psych ward if need be. What in the heck was wrong with her? She so wasn't this flustered girl. She'd been avoiding Kyle as if he were carrying an infectious disease.

But from the second she'd stepped into that damn observation room and had seen him lying back in that chair, his eyes closed, his body relaxed, his no-touch attitude more than apparent, she'd been on edge. Though there'd been at least a dozen people between them, she'd felt as if a magnet had been pulling her to him. She'd refused to look his way—that was until she passed by him, nearly making it to the exit.

Then she'd had to tumble and fall into the man's lap. And his reaction to that tumble had been more than obvious, and her body had responded in a way she couldn't remember happening before.

She was a doctor for goodness sake. She knew how the system worked, knew it was normal to feel attraction, to have all the chemicals mix together to make one person desire another. It was the way to insure the species would survive. Sex was essential to mankind.

Sex was a need as simple as hunger or thirst. She'd experimented in college, but she'd never been able to get past analyzing every little thing she was feeling, so she'd determined that sex was nothing more than a necessary evil to keep the world producing children. She didn't understand the billions and billions of dollars that were put into selling sex. It was messy and unsatisfying. Maybe it was only good for a guy. Her college boyfriend had seemed pleased with the act and himself.

She'd been left wanting.

But as she'd felt Kyle's thickness push against her ass, she'd been having thoughts that had nothing to do with medical musings. No. She'd been hot, and her body had responded, all her blood rushing from her brain to one choice place, and she had to fight not to spread her thighs and push a little closer to him.

It had to be pure animal instinct.

The need to do that had been the final push she'd needed to break the connection of his eyes. Damn, those eyes were endless brown depths of passion and secrets. They invited a person in, and Patsy wasn't sure she'd be able to escape if she accepted the invitation he seemed to be offering.

Patsy was focused on her job, she had to remind herself. She was focused and ready, and she didn't have time for men. That was the plan. And even if she did have the time, it would never be with someone as arrogant and self-centered as Dr. Kyle Armistead. Not a chance she'd sleep with a man like him. He was totally the love 'em and leave 'em guy. And she didn't do what most med students did, getting pleasure in ten-minute increments between cases.

She had chosen her profession because of her love of medicine, not to sleep with every available male there. She could keep her hormones at bay and hopefully forget all about her boss. Easy peasy. She was feeling better already.

In her need to get out of the hospital, she rounded a corner and ran smack dab into the middle of a hard chest. She would've gone straight onto her ass if it weren't for the strong arms that quickly enveloped her.

"Where's the fire?" the male voice asked.

Patsy looked up and took in a breath.

Damn!

Were all the medical personnel in this hospital downright gorgeous? Was she on an episode of Grey's Anatomy? She was in Seattle so that could very well be. She almost called the man Dr. McSteamy—barely managing to stop herself. That show had failed the world when they killed off that man. What a true tragedy for all human kind.

"Are you okay?" he asked. She stood there dumbfounded as she tried to form words. An awkward moment or two passed before she was able to shake off her nervousness.

"Sorry. I'm getting lost in my own head this afternoon, and not paying attention to where I'm going. Apparently I'm not doing to well at speaking either," she told him sheepishly.

He laughed, the sound full of good humor. She gazed at his beautiful face and wondered why her body wasn't reacting to this man as it had to Kyle. They were equally gorgeous, and both smelled incredibly good. It made no sense to her. Maybe it was back to her medical musings and the desire for the species to continue and her body wasn't calling to this man's body. Maybe something in their DNA wasn't suited. Who knew? She was so lost in her thoughts she forgot she was standing in front of him.

"Are you one of the new residents?" the doctor asked.

"Yes, Patsy Lander, Plastic Surgeon Resident," she said, holding out a hand. He took it, and she didn't feel a smidgeon of a spark. Darn it.

"Dr. Kian Forbes. I'm in trauma and agreed to teach your group, so I'll be calling you down a lot," he said, an easy smile resting on his lips.

"Kian, are you harassing residents again?" a woman's voice asked. She stepped up and Patsy was stunned at the beauty of the woman. With plastic surgery as her specialty she definitely noticed gorgeous people. When the woman was next to Dr. Forbes it was like a magazine ad come to life with the two of them.

"I'd never harass anyone, darling," Kian said with a look full of adoration toward the woman at his side. Patsy was glad she hadn't felt any attraction to the doctor. She would've felt guilty since they were obviously head over heels in love.

"Hi. I'm Roxie Forbes, this man's wife. I've been trying to get him out of here for the past hour but he's popular today," Roxie said with a laugh. She didn't seem at all put out that she was waiting for her husband.

"I'm Patsy Lander and I've only been here a week, so if I'm not physically lost then I'm so focused on my thoughts that I might as well be in a dark tunnel. It's my fault Dr. Forbes is late. I nearly ran him down," she said.

"What's your specialty?" Roxie asked, seeming genuinely interested.

"Plastic surgery," Patsy told her.

Roxie's grin grew. "Then you'll be working with Kian a lot. There's so much trauma that comes in the ER, and he makes sure to call you guys right away, especially if it's facial wounds."

"That's what I love about my field. We have the chance to change a person's future," Patsy told them. She had to consciously keep herself from reaching out and touching her own chest where she'd had surgery. Sure, it wasn't a scar most of the world saw, but it was something she looked at every day when she stripped for a shower. It mattered that it didn't disfigure her.

"Why does your name sound so familiar?" Kian asked.

Patsy shrugged, a little embarrassed. People didn't recognized the name from her. When your sister marries one of the most eligible bachelors in Seattle, people tended to remember the name. She didn't want to go into that though.

"It's sort of common," she said.

Kian shrugged as if it was no big deal. She was grateful. She wanted to do well on her own, not because of who her in-laws were. She loved the Titans, and would do anything for any of them. She wouldn't, however, take advantage of who they were.

"I better get going. It was wonderful to meet you both," Patsy said. After just a few moments of speaking to them she found she liked them.

"Definitely a pleasure," Roxie told her, looking as if she meant it.

"I'll be seeing you around, kid," Dr. Forbes said. Some people might have taken offense to the word kid, but Pasty found it a term of endearment. She smiled and walked away.

Maybe it wasn't going to be so bad working at the hospital after all. She could get over her strange feelings toward Dr. Armistead. She was strong—always had been, always would be. Her feelings toward someone wasn't going to change her course of action. No way, no how.

She convinced herself she was feeling better already. Within a few days, surely she'd believe it.

CHAPTER SIX

KYLE HAD A feeling he wasn't going to shake off his attraction to his newest resident. Not a chance in hell. He'd been intrigued by her the second her beast of a dog used him as a step ladder, and the cool way she'd blown him off had brought out the hunter instincts within him.

He thought he could get over it. That's what he should do for damn sure. He was her boss. There was no possible way for this to end well. On top of that, she was innocent. She might want to hide that with quirky little one-liners, but he could see the naiveté in her eyes.

That meant she was off limits.

His pants tightened as he thought about her on his lap. She'd been as turned on as he was; there was something between them he hadn't felt in a very long time.

Could he honestly ignore that?

Could he afford not to?

The answer was no, he couldn't afford to ignore something so powerful. He picked up his pace as he walked the long corridors of the hospital. But he did have a job to do, so maybe it would be smart to call one of the many females who'd be grateful to go out with him. The ones who didn't have expectations.

A girl like Patsy wasn't one you waited two weeks to call again. She was a roses-and-chocolates female—the one who ended up with a white picket fence—his absolute nightmare.

Kyle turned the corner and saw Patsy; his pep talk flew out the window. He stood back and watched as she talked to Kian Forbes, the best damn trauma surgeon in the Northwest, possibly the United States. Kyle respected the man, respected his entire family. This was a great place to work and Kyle would be a fool to mess that up with a tawdry affair that was bound to bite him in the ass.

Even with all this knowledge, he watched as the conversation ended and Patsy moved to the locker room—the co-ed locker room. He should turn around and walk away. That would most definitely be the smart decision.

He moved forward instead. He wasn't always known to think with his upper brain.

Telling himself his shift was finished and he needed to head home, didn't do him a lick of good. He could've waited a few minutes for her to leave the room. But he didn't.

He didn't even pause before stepping inside—where he found her alone. His pulse accelerated.

"I thought this hospital was a lot bigger than it obviously is," Patsy said with a touch of disdain, as she looked right at him. At least she wasn't ignoring him. He was now figuring out sarcasm was her way of protecting herself when she was uncomfortable.

"The walls tend to shrink in on us when we're not looking," he told her. "It's a bit like living in an *Alice in Wonderland* world.

Instead of moving to his locker, he walked over to her, wondering what he was doing. This was insane. It was almost as if he had no control over himself. One thing he knew for sure was he enjoyed how his body responded in the presence of this woman.

"I'm going home. It's been a long week," she said. She was looking at her locker before glancing at him sideways. They were all doctors. They saw naked people every single day, which was why a co-ed room wasn't so bad, but he found himself holding his breath as he watched her trying to decide if she was going to change in front of him.

He wasn't sure he'd be able to keep his hands off her if she did. Doctor or not, there were times the human body was only a canvas needing paint—and times it was for sex.

She grabbed her clothes and stuffed them in a bag, choosing to save them both and remain in her scrubs. He was definitely disappointed.

"Are you hungry?" he asked, not sure who was more surprised—her or him.

"No," she told him after a few silent moments.

He smiled, hearing the lie in her voice. They had to grab food whenever they could when they were on shift, and he knew for sure they were hungry all the time. It was the profession. When they were at work they didn't have a life outside of their job, including time to eat.

"Want to get a coffee?" he asked. What was wrong with him? He seriously couldn't seem to stop himself.

She looked at him as if she was asking herself the exact same question in her own mind. Did he enjoy the constant refusal of the woman?

"No. We work together, let's keep it to that," she told him.

He smiled. She had no idea her constant refusal was only fueling him more. He couldn't ever remember being turned down by a woman, not since he'd hit puberty at least. It was almost euphoric.

"We might as well get a dinner over with, discover this attraction between us is bound to fizzle, and then get on with our lives," he said, feeling he sounded perfectly reasonable. "We could skip the meal if you want and just head to the closest on-call room."

She glared at him, looking as if she wanted to push him over the bench he was standing in front of. He vowed he'd take her with him. Then they could be horizontal. That was quite appealing.

She opened her mouth to say something when the door opened and four residents stepped inside, their conversation loud and animated. They didn't seem to notice Kyle and Patsy awkwardly standing there.

He turned away from Patsy, trying to figure out his next move. He only looked away for a couple of seconds, but when he returned his attention to where she'd been standing, all he saw was empty space.

He looked toward the door in time to see it shutting . . . with her on the other side of it. He considered chasing her down, but thought it was probably best she'd ditched him. He obviously wasn't thinking with his bigger brain—not around her.

Maybe he needed to visit his brothers again. Not that they'd give him any solid advice. They sure as hell hadn't so far.

Patsy was just one more resident in a long line of them, and if Kyle wanted to figure out what in the hell he was trying to accomplish, he'd be wise to stay away from her. She'd be here and then she'd be gone. He'd dealt with more difficult situations in his life than an attraction to the wrong woman.

As he left the hospital he could almost swear he smelled her sweet perfume in the hallways. He shook his head as he tried holding his breath. Whatever didn't kill him would surely make him stronger, he assured himself.

CHAPTER SEVEN

SOMETHING WAS WRONG. Kyle knew it the second he stepped outside. It was dark and misty, which was normal for Seattle. But there was a touch of dread in the air. He'd always trusted his instincts and he paused as he listened, his eyes searching the hospital parking lot.

Normally he didn't park in this area, but he'd been late to work and had taken the first available space. Right now, though, something kept him from moving forward. He waited.

Then he heard a scream. His body froze as he tried to figure out where it was coming from. This was a hospital. Injured people arrived all the time, people in pain. A scream was nothing to be afraid of. But there was something about that sound; it was more terror than pain.

"I warned you to save her," a man yelled.

Kyle began moving.

"Sir, please let us talk to you. Just calm down and let's go inside." Kyle's step faltered. He knew that voice well. It was Patsy, and she was foolish enough to try to reason with an obviously unstable man.

"You have nothing to do with this. Stay the hell out of my way," the man screamed, his voice shaking. He wasn't in a rational frame of mind—a mind that could be reasoned with.

Kyle moved faster. He couldn't yet see Patsy or the man, or whoever was with them, but he'd get through the vehicles and find them. Patsy was obviously in trouble, and there was no way he was sitting back.

"I just want to help you," Patsy said.

"I'm so sorry about your wife," another woman said. Kyle didn't recognize her voice.

"You lying bitch," the man screamed.

Kyle's heart stopped when two gunshots rang out and Patsy screamed.

"Look what you made me do!" the man yelled. Then there was another gunshot, then silence.

Kyle ran and turned a corner. He found Patsy and another woman on the ground, both of them covered in blood. Several feet away a man lay on the ground as well, a bloody hole in his head, his body completely still, a black handgun lying a couple of feet from him.

Kyle moved to the gun and kicked it farther away. The guy wasn't moving, but Kyle wasn't taking any chances. Then he rushed over to Patsy and she looked up, terror and pain in her expression. His heart thudded as he leaned down, running his hands over her in rapid movements.

"Where are you hit?" he asked, his phone out as he pushed a button.

The ER reception picked up after the first ring, and he shouted a command of where they were before dropping the phone and grabbing Patsy again.

She opened and closed her mouth as if she was in shock, then looked at the woman next to her curled into a ball crying. He didn't recognize her. Finally, after what felt like an eternity, Patsy spoke.

"I wasn't hit. Dr. Wasp was. He shot her twice, once in the abdomen and once in the thigh," Patsy said. That's when he finally noticed Patsy was holding her hand over the groaning woman's stomach. She was losing too much blood.

Kyle reached for the wound on her leg and applied pressure. Everything in him wanted to run his hands over Patsy again, to ensure himself she hadn't been hit by any stray bullets. He glanced the man's way several times to make sure he indeed wasn't a threat any longer. The guy didn't move. Kyle would be shocked if he wasn't dead.

The hospital crew arrived in record time, and things moved quickly. Neither Patsy nor Kyle were trauma surgeons, but they could help in a pinch. That wasn't necessary when they were only a few dozen yards from the ER entrance.

"What happened here?" Dr. Kian Forbes asked as he quickly assessed all four people with a visual before deciding who needed the most help.

"I was walking out with Dr. Wasp when this man approached. He held the gun and started shouting at Dr. Wasp, saying she'd killed his wife. Then he pointed the gun at her. I tried to talk him down but he was beyond listening," Patsy said.

Her adrenaline was wearing down, and she began shaking from the terror of what had just happened.

"Are you hit?" Kian asked.

"No. Dr. Wasp was hit in the abdomen and thigh. Then the man shot himself in the head. Neither Dr. Armistead nor I were hit," Patsy told him.

"I'll need you to stay and talk to the police," Kian told her.

She nodded, but Kyle wasn't sure if she had heard much of what he'd said.

"Did you see anything?" Kian asked him.

"No. I walked out and heard shouting then heard the shots, but I didn't see any of it. I got here after the man was dead," Kyle told him.

"Okay, the cops will need your statement as well," Kian told him.

"Of course," Kyle replied. "I'll take Patsy in to get cleaned up, then we'll be in the cafeteria. Tell them to find us there."

"It might be a while. That's a good idea," Kian said.

Then the man turned away from both of them as he went inside with Dr. Wasp. The gunman was pronounced dead and a couple staff members waited with his covered body for the police to arrive. This was officially a crime scene.

Kyle helped Patsy to her feet, and she was shaking as he placed his arm around her. He was amazed at how composed she was, considering what she'd just been through. She didn't say a word as he began walking her inside the hospital, but she didn't push him away.

They made it to the thankfully empty locker room and he found a quiet corner and sat down, pulling her onto his lap. By now blood was splattered over both of them, but he didn't care. He'd had blood covering him many times before.

"It's okay, Patsy. You can let it out," Kyle told her.

Almost as if she'd needed permission, a shudder ran through her, and tears fell down her cheeks as she allowed herself to rest against him. Kyle rubbed her back and had to push down the rage toward the person who'd threatened her. Every instinct in him wanted to go and pulverize the man. He couldn't get that satisfaction though, as the coward had taken his own life.

"I'm sorry," she said after only a couple of minutes. She pulled herself together far more quickly than many people would've been able to do.

"You have nothing to apologize for," he assured her.

She shook her head, took in a shuddery breath, then pushed against him. Kyle didn't want to let her go, but he wasn't going to force her to take his comfort.

She got up and moved away from him before turning back and looking at him. "No, I shouldn't have fallen apart like that. I'm a doctor, and it's my job to be strong in an emergency."

Kyle stood as he let out a laugh with no humor. "We're not just doctors. We're also human beings, and I'd have to wonder about anyone who has a gun pointed at them and doesn't freak out," he offered.

"He wasn't after me," Patsy reminded him.

"It doesn't matter. You were there, and you were trying to stop it. You could've gotten yourself killed." He wasn't sure why that upset him so much. He didn't know this woman. Yes, he was attracted to her, but they were nothing to each other.

"I'd hate myself if I'd have walked away. Could you have?" she asked.

Kyle wanted to lie to her, tell her that yes, he could've left. It wasn't his business or his problem. "No, I wouldn't have walked away either."

"Then don't expect me to." She stopped, sighed, and walked back to him. She shocked him when she leaned up, wrapped her arms around him and gave him a hug that melted his cold heart a little. "Thank you for being there, for helping me."

He reached around her to pull her in tighter and she released her grip and stepped back. She seemed as if she wanted to say more so he waited. She took another step away before talking again.

"I'm going to clean up. You probably should too. I don't think either of us is getting out of here for a while." There was such weariness in her expression and body he wanted to do something for her, but he didn't know what.

She didn't wait for his response as she moved to her locker and grabbed spare scrubs. He realized they'd forgotten to grab her bag from the parking lot. He'd call down and ask for it. He was sure someone in the ER had it. But he needed to clean up as well. They each grabbed a fresh set of scrubs and moved their separate ways to the showers.

Kyle was a mess at the thought of Patsy in a shower only a few feet away from him. He heard the water turn on and all thoughts of danger evaporated in an instance. He felt like the worst sort of pig at having lustful thoughts about her after what she'd just gone through.

He switched the water to cold and leaned his head against the wall of the tile shower and counted to about a hundred before he gave up. The day had been long; the night was going to be longer. But he was glad he'd been there.

They finished about the same time and Kyle met her outside the locker room, unable to be in there with her any longer without doing something utterly foolish. She gave him a slight smile as if she was grateful for his restraint.

He was going to make love to this woman—there was zero doubt in his mind.

There was no more debate about it anymore. He wished he could walk away, wished he wasn't being such a fool when it came to her. But he knew it was going to happen. What he didn't know was how much it was going to change his life.

Even if he knew what the final outcome would be, he could do nothing to stop it at this point. She'd gotten to him, and he didn't want to hold back any longer.

He *refused* to stop it.

Now he had to see where in the hell it was all leading. If he were a smarter man he'd cut ties right now. But it seemed as if Kyle was making all sorts of life-changing decisions lately. He didn't see any reason to stop that now.

CHAPTER EIGHT

PATSY NORMALLY DIDN'T allow people to care for her. She was strong and stubborn, and because of her childhood she had learned to take care of herself. Sure, she had a sister who was incredible, who had raised her because their father had been an absolute piece of crap. But Patsy had wanted to find her independence, wanted to prove she was fine on her own.

But tonight it had been so easy to lean on Kyle. She didn't know this man, or at least she knew very little about him. She was frustrated at how attracted she was to him. And she hated how she'd fallen apart in his arms.

She also couldn't help but smile as she sat across from him in a corner of the hospital cafeteria drinking coffee. She'd told him no to dinner, and no to coffee, and yet there she was with a tray of untouched food in front of her and a coffee in her hand.

"People don't often tell you no, do they?" she asked.

He looked at her and smiled, the first real smile she'd seen since, well, probably since the day Eeyore had jumped all over him. It was hard to resist a man who loved a dog—especially her dog who she thought was pretty dang incredible.

"No, not really," he admitted. He reached down and picked up his sandwich, taking a bite.

She looked at her own food as if it was covered in mold. Eating was the last thing she wanted to do, but she was also a doctor and knew she needed the fuel. She picked up a chip and popped it in her mouth, having no clue what flavor it was.

"Well, I wouldn't be here now if I didn't have to be," she told him. The fear from the night was wearing off, and she was finding her voice again.

"Why do you say that?" he asked. His food was a third of the way gone already. The longer time went on, the calmer she felt. Her appetite started coming back. She picked up her slice of pizza and took a bite, glad she was able to taste the spice of the peperoni.

"Because I told you we weren't doing dinner," she reminded him.

"This isn't our date, Patsy. That will come when this is all over," he assured her.

She took another bite and narrowed her eyes. "I appreciate confident people, but delusional is another matter altogether," she said.

She was shocked when he leaned back and laughed. It felt wrong to be having this conversation, to be . . . flirting with this man when she'd just watched a woman get shot.

Patsy hadn't met Dr. Wasp before that night, but she was another female doctor and a nice woman. Patsy should be more worried, should be more upset. They'd already checked on her, and it looked like Dr. Wasp was going to pull through surgery just fine. Maybe that's why Patsy wasn't more upset, she assured herself. The bullet hadn't hit any major organs and they'd gotten to her in record time thanks to Kyle's quick phone call that Patsy had been too shocked to make.

"I've been called worse than delusional before, so go ahead and hit me with your best shot," he told her.

She finished her pizza and grabbed the chocolate cupcake on her tray. Kyle had loaded her tray down, and she was impressed with what was on it. He didn't know her, but he'd pretty much picked exactly what she'd normally have taken. That should terrify her a little, especially since he had different food on his own tray.

She looked at her food, then his, then away.

"I've seen you eating in here a few times," he told her, reading her mind.

"Do you like stalking residents?" she asked.

"Normally I don't care much at all about residents. I had my own practice for ten years but spent a lot of time in hospitals doing surgeries and consulting with other doctors. Now I'm a teacher and, of course, I take more of an interest," he said.

"Including our food choices?" she questioned.

"I only notice the food choices of the residents I plan on taking to my bed," he said conversationally.

Patsy choked on the sip of coffee she'd just taken.

Kyle sat back and smiled.

"That's so not going to happen," she told him.

His expression didn't change. "Yes, it will, but I'll give you time to adjust to the reality of it."

"That's so magnanimous of you," she said with a glare.

"I'm a good guy," he assured her. "I'm always thinking about others."

Patsy wanted to fight the smile trying to break free, but she couldn't quite push it all the way down.

"I've yet to meet a surgeon who doesn't think they're God," she told him.

He grinned back as he sipped his coffee, looking disappointed when his cup was empty. "That's because we play God every time we're in the OR."

"Even when doing a pair of boobs?" she challenged.

He laughed harder this time, and she couldn't keep her own smile away. "Hell yeah, when doing boobs. Those are highly important to mankind's existence," he assured her as his eyes trailed down her throat and landed on her own chest. She desperately wanted to cross her arms but wasn't giving him that satisfaction.

"Mine are one hundred percent real," she said instead as if she didn't care that he was looking at her.

His gaze slowly traveled back to her face and his grin grew as he licked his lips in a way that had heat coursing down her body and throbbing in one particular place she didn't normally pay attention to. She tried not to squirm in her seat.

"That's more than obvious," he said in a husky voice.

She was saved from the conversation continuing when two officers approached. They gave their statements together, and Patsy wasn't sure if she was glad or not to be pulled away from her conversation with the man.

He intrigued her, which scared the crud out of her. She had to remind herself she didn't have the time or the desire to have a workplace affair—especially with an arrogant surgeon.

When she was paged to the ER, letting her know they had her bag, she ran like the chicken she was. If she continued her intimate conversation with Kyle, she was afraid she was going to do exactly what he'd said they were going to do and fall into his bed.

That would make life incredibly awkward the next day at work. As she hailed a cab and went home, she told herself she was being smart. If she'd fallen at the feet of every doctor who'd flirted with her from the day she'd stepped into this program, she'd have far too many notches on her bedpost. And she reminded herself she didn't like sex; it was boring and messy.

But if that was truly the case why in the hell was she feeling strong urges toward Kyle she'd never felt toward another man before? And why was her body so out of sync, so needy? And why, as she made her way home, was loneliness seeping through her normally content life? She wondered if it was okay to let down her guard every once in a while.

She wondered if she was missing out on something essential because she was too worried to live.

CHAPTER NINE

FAMILY BARBEQUES WERE mandatory when it came to the Titan family. Patsy had been able to avoid them for a while because she was a resident working incredibly long hours. But she did have a rare Sunday off, and the pleading from her sister had been enough to guilt her into going.

It wasn't that she didn't love hanging out with her sister. But Nicole had a way of reading her like an open book, and the second she took a look at Patsy's face she was going to know something was up.

Patsy hoped her acting skills would be up to the task of getting through a family event. She did miss her sister and the wonderful family she'd married into, especially since Nicole and Patsy's family had been so far from perfect there weren't words to compare how bad it had been.

That was all in the past, and their futures had been drastically changed. A lot of that had to do with Ryan, Patsy's amazing brother-in-law. He treated Nicole like the princess she was, and he looked at Patsy as if she were his little sister. It made her feel loved but a little bit smothered. However that was better than the alternative. It was much better to have people who loved you too much, versus having no one care or know where you were or what you were doing.

Walking up to her brother-in-law's house, Patsy took a deep breath, knowing the interrogation was coming. Then she let out a laugh. From the way her thoughts were going, people would think her family were nothing but tyrants. That was far from the truth. They were loving and loyal and she was acting foolish.

She opened the door and made her way into the living room where the entire family was waiting. Nicole looked up, her eyes sparkling as she jumped from the sofa, handing over the baby in her arms to her equally smiling husband.

"I've been waiting all day," Nicole said as she ran and threw her arms around Patsy.

Why she'd avoided coming home she'd never know because she loved this woman with all her heart.

"I'm sorry. I've been so busy," Patsy said.

"Just don't ever be too busy for family," Nicole scolded.

"I promise I'll do better," Patsy assured her.

"Good," Ryan said as he walked up, baby Jesse in his arms. "Your sister starts to go stir crazy when she doesn't get to see you or talk to you."

"I've missed you guys," Patsy assured him. She looked from Nicole to Ryan. Then she held out her hands. "Now give me my nephew."

Ryan handed over the two-month-old baby and Patsy cooed at him. He smiled at her, and she knew he already held her heart in his hands.

"He's growing too fast," Patsy told them with a frown.

"Babies tend to grow when you're not looking," Nicole said with a chuckle. "And since this will be our last, we plan to enjoy him for as long as we can."

"Don't say that. I want a dozen nieces and nephews," Patsy told her sis as she moved into the room and sat down with the baby in her arms.

Nicole laughed again. "I don't think any of us can handle me pregnant that many times. I'm a bit of a diva."

Ryan laughed. "I don't mind middle of the night Taco Bell runs," he assured her.

"Or me getting fat?" Nicole asked with a twinkle in her eyes.

His expression went serious. "You are beautiful, Nicole, pregnant, not pregnant, young or old, fat or thin. There's nothing you could do that would change how I see you."

Patsy's eyes filled with tears at the pure adoration in Ryan's eyes and voice. He meant what he said. He was so in love with his wife there was nothing she could do he wouldn't consider spectacular.

"I love you, Ryan."

"I love you, Nic," he replied before giving her a kiss.

"Okay, for those of us who are single, this is a bit disgusting," Patsy said.

Nicole's head turned to the side as she looked at her sister, and Patsy squirmed in her seat. She knew that look well. She gazed at her nephew and hoped like heck Nicole wasn't zeroing in on her.

"I know that tone of voice, sis," Nicole said. "I also see the blush you're trying to hide." She moved closer. "Have you met a man at work?"

Patsy's cheeks heated more as all eyes in the room turned to her.

"Oh, I should have popcorn right now. Nic's on to something," Jasmine piped in. She'd been silent so far.

Jasmine was married to Derek Titan, Ryan's cousin. Though Ryan, Derek, and Drew were cousins, they were far more like brothers than cousins, and their families were always together. When the three wives got together there was no stopping them when they wanted to know something.

Derek was the one to chuckle now. "You might as well spill because you know they're going to continue to grill you until you tell all."

Patsy glared at the man she considered an uncle. They'd been in her life since she was a little girl when Nic started dating Ryan. Patsy had been devastated when they'd broken up. She'd been overjoyed when they got back together again. It hadn't been an easy road for the two of them, but it didn't matter. They were together now and more in love than ever before; at the end of the day that was all that mattered.

"There's nothing to tell," Patsy said. "I think Jesse needs a diaper change, though." Hopefully they'd focus on her beautiful nephew instead of her.

"Don't try to change the subject. We're definitely on to something here," Nicole said as she moved closer.

"I like a good grilling," Trinity spoke up.

Trinity was married to the youngest cousin, Drew, and Patsy had always felt a special bond with her. She looked at her with a pleading glance and Trinity laughed.

"I can't help you, kid, not on this one. I'm too curious," Trinity said in betrayal. Patsy huffed.

"Okay, okay," she said. "But Jesse really does need changed. I'll take care of it." She began to stand when Nic held up a hand.

Ryan laughed as he came over and took Jesse. "Looks like I'm on dad duty so your sister can get a tell-all from you," he said. He looked at his son like he was the most precious thing in the world.

If Patsy could be with a man who looked at her the way Ryan looked at his wife and children, maybe she'd consider a real relationship. But even though Ryan truly would love his wife no matter what, Patsy was very aware of her internal scars from past trauma. She was worried a man wouldn't see past that. Her college lover certainly hadn't cared enough to see past a single thing, not even the small mark on her chest. That mark told her she was alive, but many men wanted utter perfection.

"There is a doctor I have a slight crush on, but it can't go anywhere, so I don't see a need to talk about it. It's sort of why I've avoided you the past couple of weeks. You seem to have radar anytime a man comes anywhere near me," Patsy said with a long sigh.

Nicole's mouth gaped. "I just care about you and want the best," she assured her sister.

"I know you do, Nic. But everything in my life's changing, and I don't really know what to say about any of it," Patsy told her.

Nicole looked as if she didn't know what to say herself, a first for her sister. That made Patsy grin.

"I just want you to be happy. That's all I've ever wanted."

Patsy rose from her chair and crossed to her sister, throwing her arms around her as tears sparkled in her eyes. They didn't say a word for several moments before Patsy pulled back.

"I know you do. You've done so much for me my entire life, sacrificed way too much. I would die for you." She paused as she took a deep breath. "But you have to let me grow up and trust that I'm okay. I'll make smart choices in life and dumb ones, but I'll be okay either way."

Nicole looked as if she wanted to argue with that statement, but Ryan stepped back into the room with a happy baby in his arms. He passed Jesse to Jasmine, who gladly took him, then placed an arm around both Nicole and Patsy.

"Your sister will work on letting you grow up," he assured her.

Patsy laughed and he looked confused. "What about you, my sweet brother-in-law? Are you going to let me grow up?" she challenged.

He shrugged his shoulders sheepishly. "I'll do my best," he said. Then as if he was trying to act nonchalant, which he didn't pull off well, he tried to make his next question casual. "Who is this doctor you're speaking of?"

Patsy laughed heartily as she gave Ryan a big hug before pulling away. He waited and she kept him that way for a few long seconds.

"There's not a chance I'm giving you that information. You'll have his entire background and social security number within an hour," she said. Kyle hadn't done anything to deserve the Titan men coming after him—at least not yet.

"More like half an hour," Drew piped in.

"Probably have his weight at birth by then too," Derek said with his own laugh.

"You're not helping," Ryan said, glaring at his cousins.

"None of you are helping in any way. I know your meddling is done with love, but I'm a big girl now, and if I choose to ever date again, I'm not telling any of you about it."

That earned her scowls from all three men and laughter from their wives.

"You've grown up so much in such a short time," Nic said, her tone proud.

"Because you raised me well," Patsy told her. She had to wipe a tear away.

Their father had been an abusive alcoholic, and if it hadn't been for Nicole, Patsy couldn't imagine how her life would've turned out. She truly was grateful for her sister and all she'd done.

The smiles fell away and Patsy knew what was coming next. Her sister took a deep breath and brushed the hair behind her ears. This was what Pasty had hoped wouldn't happen.

"Now that we got men and not enough visits out of the way . . ." Nicole began.

"I'm sorry, Nic," Pasty said as she twisted in her seat.

"How in the world did we hear second hand that you were shot at?" Nic said, tears popping into her eyes.

Pasty felt lower than a sewer rat for hurting her sis.

"I wasn't actually shot at and I didn't want you to worry," Patsy said. "It was a very unhappy husband with one of our doctors who had done nothing wrong. I was just in the wrong place at the wrong time. But I'm glad I was there because she made it through and is doing fine now."

"A gun was pointed at you," Nic said, tears falling down her face.

"I promise if anything like that happens again, I'll call you immediately. I really am sorry, sis," Patsy said as she sat next to her sister and threw her arms around her.

Nicole sniffled for a minute as she held tightly to Patsy. Then she leaned back and gave a wobbly smile.

"We've always told each other everything. Don't exclude me from your life," Nic pleaded.

"You're my everything, Nic. It won't happen again," Pasty assured her.

They hugged for a long time and then thankfully Ryan saved the day from the emotional moment.

"Okay, we've got the grilling done, now let's have some food and drinks," he said with a sly smile.

Patsy laughed again, glad to feel the heartache dissipate. "If you think you'll get me drunk so I'll talk, think again," she told her brother-in-law. She ignored his grumble as she made her way to the back deck where enough food to feed a small army was set up.

She was glad to be home. Even the interrogation was worth it. For just a little while her worries faded away and all was right with the world.

CHAPTER TEN

L IFE WAS ABOUT goals. Yes, there were struggles mixed in there, but at the end of the day, you wanted to be able to look in the mirror and know who you were and where you were going. People would come and go in your life, but there was no chance of outrunning yourself. There was no escaping your destiny—not ever.

Patsy was glad to remember those simple facts. Kyle wouldn't be a permanent fixture in her life, so she was happy to get back to doing what she'd always wanted to do. She was even more grateful when he wasn't hovering around her through the next week of her residency.

Because she wanted to focus more on emergency medicine, helping those rushed into an ER with a bite wound to the face, a nose slashed off, or a chemical burn, she got to know Dr. Kian Forbes a lot more, which was a bonus.

She liked him. He was so damn knowledgeable. But above that he was patient and kind, and she thanked her lucky stars he gave her the time of day and his expertise.

A lot of plastic surgeons wanted to move to a big city and perform ten-thousand-dollar breast implants since that paid so much more than fixing a jagged scar on someone's face, but at the end of the day Patsy wanted to look herself in the mirror and be proud of who she was.

Of course, that's what she'd always thought. That was until she had some good insight from a great surgeon. Maybe it was time to be less judgmental of which areas of medicine doctors chose to practice.

Just because someone wanted to change something about their body didn't make them vain, didn't make them a bad person. She was beginning to realize no one was ever truly happy with who they were. That was what made people want to be better. And it wasn't her place or anyone else's place to decide on what someone chose to do to themselves.

Who was she to judge anyone when she had her own demons?

"You've learned a lot. That's what will make you great at your job," Kian told her as the two of them observed a mother on the operating table with a deep laceration in her chest from a drug deal gone wrong. She had stabilized, and the internal wounds had been dealt with, so it was time to fix the outside. Sometimes it was easy to cast blame on the life a person had chosen to live. That wasn't Patsy's job though.

"I've been pretty judgmental," Patsy admitted.

Kian shrugged, giving her a kind smile. "We've all had those days. I've had people on my table high on meth with their foot hanging halfway off because they decided to play with fireworks or an ax. I've had pregnant mothers with wounds in their stomachs because they were so drunk they fell down a flight of stairs. I've had my moments of outrage and entitlement thinking I was too good a doctor to treat someone who didn't care enough to take care of themselves. But I learned that I don't know their story. I don't know what got them to that point in life. All I know is I made a vow to help everyone, not judge them. And if I show kindness to someone, it might change their life in a better way. Maybe not, but it's not my place to choose who is worthy of care and who isn't. We're all human, and we all make mistakes."

"I guess I still have a lot to learn," Patsy admitted.

"We all do," Kian told her.

Patsy felt a certain tingling down her spine before looking up. She told herself not to do it, she was being foolish. But as she held a scalpel in her fingers, she couldn't stand the feeling anymore so her eyes were drawn to the observation windows.

And there he was.

As much as she wanted to tell herself she didn't like Kyle Armistead, she was drawn to him so much that she could feel him before seeing him. He was standing there, his eyes fixed on her as she worked.

She had barely caught glances of him through the week after the shooting, and the sight of him was enough to take her breath away, enough to make her mess up her surgery. She had to look away quickly before Dr. Forbes and the rest of the staff saw how affected she was.

But even as she focused once more on her patient, she couldn't help the image that had been burned in her brain. He looked so damn good in his green scrubs with his soulful eyes looking at her with what appeared to be approval.

He was new to this hospital just as she was, and there seemed to be a hint of unease in his eyes as if he wasn't quite sure of his own journey. Were the two of them lost souls seeking each other? Had they already bonded in a way that couldn't be broken?

That was absolutely ridiculous, she chided herself.

"Is everything okay, Dr. Lander?" Kian asked.

She had to push back the tremor wanting to wrack her body. This wasn't the time or the place to think of Kyle. He was just another doctor, one of many who'd come and go in her life. He didn't matter.

"Of course. Sorry for the delay," she replied, refusing to look up again to see if Kyle had noticed her distraction.

Patsy focused on her patient, trying to ignore the bruising on the woman's face and remembering she was a person, a daughter, a mother, possibly a sister, a niece. No one chose to live a life like she'd chosen. Maybe bad choices had led to her decision, but she still deserved the best medical care, and she deserved respect. She was a human. Maybe it would change how she saw herself if they saw her as a good person. Maybe she'd choose to go down another path from this day out.

Maybe she wouldn't. That wasn't for Patsy to decide. There were a lot of stitches needed and she was grateful for the staff in the room with her, teaching her, standing by with compassion without judgment. Patsy had a lot to learn in this line of work she'd chosen.

Thankfully she had good teachers. She pushed thoughts of Kyle from her mind and worked alongside Kian as they tried to make their patient as good as new. The hours flew by and she became lost in her job.

When the surgery was finished, exhaustion filled Patsy, but a sense of pride outweighed it. The smile making her cheeks ache was also rewarding. As she began stripping her surgical garments, she knew she was where she belonged.

"You have a true gift for this," Kian said as he scrubbed his hands in the sink next to her. She was glowing at his praise.

"I've wanted to do this since I had my own surgery," she admitted, telling this man more than she had told any other medical staff.

"We all have a story about why we want to do this. If you ever want to share yours, I'm here," he said. She liked that he offered but didn't push. She was glad she'd come to this hospital.

"Thank you. I appreciate it," Patsy told him. As she finished scrubbing up she couldn't help but glance at the empty observation window for what seemed like the millionth time. Kyle had been gone a long time.

Kian's knowing gaze missed nothing. He smiled at her, and she had to fight the guilty blush wanting to steal over her. It was foolish to be crushing after one of the attending's—especially Kyle Armistead.

"Kyle hasn't been here long, but I don't often see him watching emergency surgeries," Kian pointed out, making Patsy squirm.

"I'm sure he wants to learn all the ins and outs of the hospital," Patsy told him, hoping she sounded nonchalant.

"Or he's keeping an eye on one particular doctor," Kian said with a grin that didn't try to hide what he was thinking.

"Maybe he has a crush on a nurse . . . or you," Patsy said with a slight narrowing of her eyes. She'd discovered early in her career choice that faithfulness wasn't considered mandatory in a lot of the students and doctors.

"I've heard a lot of the nurses have a crush on him," Kian said with a laugh, not offended by her tone. "And I'm not too worried he's coming after me."

"I try not to listen to gossip," Patsy told him, hoping he'd drop this conversation.

"So the rumors I've heard about sparks flying between the two of you have been false?" Kian asked. "He was pretty protective the night of shooting."

Patsy's cheeks heated, and she hated that she couldn't blame it on the temperature, since it was so cold in this particular room.

"I can't control what people say or think," Patsy said. "But I'd appreciate squashing any rumors. I have goals and an affair with my boss isn't one of them."

His grin fell away as he took a step closer, understanding in his eyes.

"I apologize if I've offended you. We work hard under stressful conditions, and sometimes a smile after a long shift makes the day a little better," Kian explained.

Patsy instantly felt like a horrible person. He was a highly successful doctor who'd been nothing but kind to her, and she was taking out her frustrations on him. Maybe she needed to lighten up a bit.

"He makes me nervous. I'm a little defensive about it," Patsy told him. "Please don't think I'm some prudish female you need to be careful what you say around," she said with a sheepish shrug.

Kian's smile returned. "I like you, Patsy. I think you're going places. My wife likes you, too. Don't think I'm easily offended. Why don't you have dinner with us on your next day off?" he asked.

"That's a little intimidating if I'm being honest," Patsy told him.

Kian laughed, making Patsy's own lips turn back up.

"I'm definitely a bad ass doctor, but you'll see how truly insignificant I am if you have dinner with us. My wife definitely runs our home," he told her with a wink.

"Now that I've told you I don't listen to gossip, you're going to know I'm a liar," she replied with her own laugh. His brows rose. "Because I've heard the Forbes family is anything other than ordinary."

He laughed again. "I guess you'll just have to come have dinner to find out," he said.

Before Patsy could say anything the pager on Kian's hip dinged, and he looked at the message before letting another chuckle escape. His entire expression changed as a love so blinding entered his eyes it made Patsy feel as if she were intruding on a private moment.

"That's my wife. I'm late again," he said.

There was only a quick goodbye after that as Kian rushed off to the lucky woman he was married to. Patsy suddenly felt very alone.

She'd seen amazing examples of love in her life. Her sister was cherished by her husband. Ryan loved her so much it was as if the universe revolved around Nicole. Her sister was a lucky woman. And Kian obviously loved his wife as she had witnessed several times.

Her uncles loved their wives too. So Patsy didn't understand why she couldn't accept that love might really exist. Probably because it hadn't always been that way for Nicole or her. Their childhood had been less than perfect. Patsy shook her head as she left the hospital. She didn't want to delve into that right now.

She'd had another successful day, and she wasn't going to let her past haunt her. Not this time—not anymore.

CHAPTER ELEVEN

KYLE DROVE HOME, exhausted after a grueling week in the hospital. He smiled as he fought down a chuckle. It had been a long time since he'd worked as hard as he'd been working these past couple of weeks.

He had no regrets giving up his practice. Money wasn't a factor in his decision. He'd been at a crossroads of where he wanted to go, and he knew he'd made the right decision. The longer it went on, the more right he knew it was.

Being with his family and in the thick of the grind was something he hadn't realized he missed, but he had indeed missed it.

If it weren't for a certain spunky young doctor, he'd think he was happy. It had been a long time since he could say that about himself. But as much as he tried to avoid her in the large hospital, he knew he was lying. He'd told her they'd be together, then he'd run away scared of how she made him feel.

If it was only sex, he could handle that. He'd desired women before—too many if he were being honest with himself. But with Patsy it wasn't just sex. She made him laugh, made him yearn for more. She made him want . . . want things he had no business wanting.

He'd sought her out earlier that day when he'd known she was assisting a surgery with Kian. She had true skill, a gift for her chosen profession. He wanted to teach her, wanted to be there as she realized her gift. Maybe he was being a fool to stay away.

Yeah, he flirted with her, and yes, he wouldn't turn her away if she dragged him into the nearest on-call room, but he wasn't willing to give more than that, and he didn't want to hurt her. Some people wanted casual—and some didn't. Patsy definitely wasn't a woman who fell into the casual territory.

Kyle parked his car and sat for a few minutes. He hated his place. He'd chosen an apartment because it was easier. He wasn't sure if he was staying in Seattle, and he didn't want to buy a house and trap himself there, but after living on the beach in California and not having to deal with noisy people all around him, it wasn't fun to come home to a cramped place.

He lived on the top floor of the building, his apartment larger than most people's homes, but he still couldn't force himself to step inside. Instead, he walked out of the garage and made his way to the front of the building, looking at the vast park in front of him—the park where he'd first met Patsy.

He wondered if she lived nearby. It made sense that she did, since they'd both been at the park. As he was thinking about that, he saw a bus stop down the road and noticed a petite woman step off it. His gut clenched. He'd recognize those legs anywhere.

His mood suddenly improved as Patsy moved closer to him, her head down as she huddled in her jacket. It might be the end of summer and the days were still warm, but the nights cooled off quickly with breezes blowing in from all the water surrounding Seattle.

She was almost to him, and he wondered if his luck was changing. It appeared she might live in the same complex he was currently in. With a satisfied grin on his lips, he waited for her to look up, to notice him.

The moment she did, she stumbled as her step faltered. Her face was expressive as she looked at him then to the double doors behind him. Her eyes narrowed.

"What are you doing here?" she asked.

"Waiting for you to invite me in for dinner," he easily told her.

Her cheeks flushed, and her mouth opened and closed as if she was trying to figure out how to respond to his words. Kyle could see she'd been raised by someone who'd taught her manners, because she was fighting with how to respond to his invitation.

"Are you serious?" she finally asked after a few long moments passed.

"If you're willing to feed me, I am," he said with an easy smile. "I'm getting sick of eating takeout and TV dinners."

She looked completely unsure of what to say next. It made her that much more endearing. He had a serious crush on this woman who looked as if she'd rather be run down by a Seattle cabbie than have dinner with him. He wondered why. Their first dinner together had been in a cafeteria with terrible food, but the conversation had been good, and he'd walked away wanting more from her—if not terrified of how he felt at the same time.

But her constant rejection was confusing because he knew he wasn't hard on the eyes, plus he was a successful doctor. He was charming and made sure his dates enjoyed their time with him. And though it had been a while since he'd had a woman in his bed, he was one hell of a lover. He couldn't remember the last time he'd been denied a date.

She took a deep breath, and her shoulders firmed. "I think this is considered stalking," she finally told him in that haughty voice that had his pants tightening as he began to throb.

He could continue the act or give her a break before she said something she was truly embarrassed about. He didn't want her to run from him—at the hospital or at their mutual residence. He had plenty of time to win this woman over. He was just surprised he wanted to. He wondered if he'd grow bored with the chase or grow more and more excited.

"I moved here a couple of weeks ago," he told her. "I assume you live here as well. I'm surprised we haven't seen each other besides that day at the park."

Her expressive eyes widened a little, making her look slightly like an anime character. That comparison made his grin widen.

He had a friend who would probably never settle down because those characters had given him an unreal expectation of what he wanted a female to look like.

"You live here?" she asked, sounding hopeful it wasn't true. His ego might've been bruised if he wasn't aware she was fighting her attraction toward him.

"Yep. It's a nice place. If you don't want to feed me, maybe I can talk you into joining me for some takeout. It's not nearly as bad with company."

"Look, Kyle, I'm very busy. I don't want to seem like a prude or rude or anything but I'm focused on my career right now, and I'm not interested in dating." She couldn't look him in the eyes. She was lying. No, she might not be interested in dating, but she liked him, and it couldn't be easy for her to keep barriers between them. He'd break her down.

"You aren't looking for friends, either?" he questioned.

Her eyes snapped to his. "Are you trying to be my friend?" she countered.

He smiled again. "For now, if that's what it takes to get you to have a meal with me," he told her. He wasn't going to lie and say that was all he wanted when he wanted so much more.

"I've got friends," she said, that haughtiness returning to her voice.

"So what can I do to get you to quit avoiding me?" he point blank asked.

Her cheeks flushed again. "I haven't been avoiding you. I've told you, I'm very busy," she said, the words trailing off as she looked at his chest. She obviously didn't like to make eye-contact when she fibbed.

"Hmm," he said, his voice a low purr. "I'm new to the city and I could certainly use a friend. I thought Seattle folks were nicer than those in California," he said. He'd do whatever it took to get what he wanted.

Her eyes snapped back to his, and he could see the wheels spinning in her head as if she was trying to figure out if he was telling the truth or not. She had compassion. He'd noticed that about her from the start. It was one of her most appealing traits. He'd use that to get to know her better.

"We work long hours. It's hard to have friendships," she said. He could see he was finally getting where he wanted to be.

"I'm not asking you to give me your firstborn," he said, loving the flush spreading down her neck at his words. "Just asking for a meal."

He wasn't sure if he wanted her to cave so easily or not. Of course, she'd been denying him for weeks, so this wouldn't exactly be caving. She placed a hand on her hip as she studied him for several more moments. Then she let out a sigh.

"I've eaten dinner—a huge dinner." She looked as if she was struggling with something. But then she firmed her resolve. "I really have to go." He didn't want to let her leave. What was wrong with him?

What he wanted was to pull her into his arms and kiss her. He wanted that more than he'd wanted anything in his entire life. It wasn't a matter of if they kissed. It was a matter of *when*.

The longer it took for it to happen, the less restraint he was going to be able to use. He was falling hard for this woman, which surprised him since he normally lost interest in the opposite sex after the first date. Maybe that's why he liked this one so much more. He was actually getting to know her a little—and so far he liked what he'd learned.

"I better let you go then," he said before stepping to the door and holding it open.

She skirted around him, making sure not a single inch of her touched him as she darted inside the building. Kyle thought about following her to the elevator, but he had to take baby steps. Maybe he should go for a run in the park. That might burn off some of his excess energy.

He waited for the elevator to close with her in it before he pressed the button and waited for the next one. He was going to change and come back down. He'd get her off his mind before he climbed into bed. But knowing she was so close would wreak havoc with his sleeping pattern. That was for dang sure.

Even with all of that Kyle was in a much better mood than he'd been in thirty minutes earlier. And it was all because Patsy Lander stirred him up, making him act and think about things he normally didn't. He was falling hard for the girl, but that wasn't something he was willing to analyze. He was simply going to enjoy how it made him feel.

He was going to enjoy her. And he was going to make sure she enjoyed him.

CHAPTER TWELVE

A S SOON AS the elevator doors closed Patsy let out a shaky breath. She hadn't dared inhale as she'd passed too closely by Kyle while entering her building. She couldn't process that he lived in the same building as she did.

Were the fates against her? She was already madly attracted to him no matter how badly she wanted to deny it. This wasn't going to help at all. How close was his apartment to hers? How had they not run into each other sooner? How was she going to sleep knowing he was within touching distance? She was in serious trouble.

Music played on the other side of her apartment door, and Patsy leaned her head against it and took a deep breath. She liked having a roommate for a couple reasons. One, she had help with her dog, so Eeyore wasn't stuck inside all day. Amber loved dogs and they worked different shifts, so she had no problem taking him to the park and letting him run off some of his energy so Patsy didn't have to board him when she worked ridiculous hours.

Two, it was sometimes scary to live alone in the city. Of course Ryan had insisted on the expensive complex, wanting her as safe as possible since she refused to live at home with him and her sister.

But there were times it wasn't quite so nice having a room-mate, and this would be one of them. Amber would take one look at Patsy's face and know something was up. She was a cursed with an open-book face. Not only that, but Amber was fairly social. She didn't often have people at the apartment, but it sounded like she had a few friends over tonight.

Hopefully they wouldn't stay too late. Patsy would exchange a few words, possibly grab a quick bite to eat since she'd lied to Kyle and she was actually starving, then she'd take Eeyore for a long walk to tucker both of them out.

She turned the knob and stepped inside. The music wasn't too loud, but the laughter seemed carefree. There were times Patsy wished she could ease up on her expectations and simply enjoy the moment like Amber did.

It wasn't like Patsy was an old lady. She was twenty-five, but while most women her age had lived a fairly exciting life, hers had been all about school and working harder and harder to achieve her goals. She wondered if one day she'd simply snap and go on a wild erotic binge.

The thought didn't sound unappealing.

Patsy walked into the room to find three people sitting at the kitchen island, snacking on chips and dip with a lot of liquor ready to be mixed. Amber turned and gave her a brilliant smile, which began to fade as she took in Patsy's expression.

"What's wrong?" Amber asked.

"Nothing's wrong. It was just a long day at work. I did get to be in the OR for six hours," she said, hoping the excitement she'd felt at assisting with the operation was showing in her voice. It definitely should and would have for sure if she hadn't been with Kyle only minutes before.

She undid her jacket, giving herself an excuse not to look at her knowing roommate. She needed to change before she walked Eeyore. Just as she had that thought, her dog came zipping around the corner, sliding on the wooden floor as he smacked into her legs, his tongue hanging as he whined up at her.

"Hello, beautiful," she said, kneeling down and scratching his head. His eyes rolled as he wiggled in front of her. She didn't need a man, she just needed her perfect dog. He was loyal, loving, and always happy to see her. He also snuggled and didn't have high expectations. Hell, he'd even seen her naked and there was no judgment in his eyes. It was true love.

"You look flushed . . ." Amber paused as if she was doing a math problem in her head. "From more than just the cold. There's something in your eyes." Her roommate was as bad as her sister. Patsy tried to figure out how to downplay this moment.

"I was talking to one of our newest neighbors," Patsy said. "He flusters me a little. That's all. No big deal." She hoped she sounded casual enough.

Amber's eyes gleamed. Her friends smiled. The dark haired one's eyes lit up.

"Oooh, you must be talking about Mr. Sexy. I ran into him this morning and decided I'm never moving from this complex. I can see why you're flustered," she said.

"You think anything with a pulse is sexy, Mindy," Amber said as she chucked a peanut at her friend.

"Not true. I have high standards," Mindy replied with a perfected pout.

"Maybe that's why you're still single. No one is quite good enough," the blonde girl said.

"And maybe your standards are too low, Alexa," Mindy replied.

None of the girls seemed offended. Amber turned her attention back to Patsy. "You look like you can use a drink." She began mixing a lemon drop, knowing it was Patsy's favorite. "Tell me why the new guy has you so flustered." There wasn't a chance Amber was dropping this so Patsy had to give her something.

"He works at the hospital with me—as my boss. He's arrogant and obviously used to getting his way. He annoys me, that's all," Patsy said, gratefully accepting the drink Amber held out.

"You've been working with Mr. Sexy and you haven't said anything?" Mindy gasped.

"There hasn't been anything to say," Patsy said with a shrug.

She handed Eeyore a piece of jerky before taking her own and biting down on it. Eeyore looked temporarily appeased while she spoke with her friends. He knew this was the routine. She'd gab for a little bit, then change, then take him out for a nice long stroll. He was a patient dog—unlike a lot of men she knew.

"That definitely means you're hiding something," Amber said, not at all buying Patsy's short explanation. "Are you totally crushing on your boss?" She seemed absolutely delighted. Of course she'd be, since Patsy had yet to bring home a guy. She wasn't into dating, and she certainly wasn't into casual hook ups.

"I admit he's cute," Patsy said, downplaying her attraction. "But he's arrogant, and in case you've forgotten, he's my boss, and I'm not going to jump into anything with him. I refuse to be another hospital tramp, willing to sleep with anyone holding a scalpel."

"You also hold a scalpel so doesn't that make you even?" Alexa asked.

"Not yet. I'm at the beginning of my career. Dr. Armistead," she said with a short pause. It was easier to talk about him more formally. Easier for her to categorize him in her mind and maybe for her roommate and friends to see she didn't like him. "Dr. Armistead," she repeated the name, "is my superior because he's been doing this a lot longer than I have. I'll get there, but it's going to take years."

"He doesn't seem that much older than you," Mindy pointed out.

"He's a plastic surgeon. Who knows how old he really is," Patsy said with a laugh.

That made the other girls laugh too. "I'm so dang glad for plastic surgery. It paid for these," Mindy said as she gripped her gorgeous breasts.

"You'll have to give me a facelift when I get old," Alexa told Patsy as she squinted her eyes. "I refuse to grow old gracefully."

"That's what I'm here for," Patsy said with a laugh. "Too bad I won't be able to perform surgery on myself." She was successfully getting them off the topic of her hot doctor . . . and neighbor.

She finished her drink and moved to the counter to mix another. One more wasn't going to make her a stumbling idiot, and she could use it after the week she'd had. She was grabbing an eggroll when Amber zeroed back in on her.

"Okay, so you say you don't like the doc, but tell us a bit about him, cause he's gorgeous, and if you don't want him, maybe I'll throw myself down the stairs in front of him so he can play doctor with me."

The instant jealousy filling Patsy at the thought of the perfect Amber flirting with Kyle made her cheeks flush again. Amber was everything Patsy wasn't: blonde, flirty, full of energy, and a guy magnet. Just because Amber was too picky to settle with any of the men chasing her, didn't mean it wasn't going to eventually happen.

Would Patsy be okay seeing Kyle in her apartment with Amber on his lap? Hell no! Everything within her rebelled at that thought. She told herself it was only because she didn't want to be around the man. But she knew that was a lie. It was pure, raw, unadulterated jealousy.

"There's not a lot to tell. He had his own practice in California, sold it, and came here. I don't know why. I haven't talked to him about it. I just listened to hospital gossip. I think his family lives here, though."

She couldn't look at Amber as she said this. Her friend read her too well, and she didn't want Amber to see the jealousy most likely residing on her face. She was a hot mess. That was for dang sure.

"I'm sure there's more to this than you're telling us, but Eeyore is about to have a heart attack waiting, so as long as you know I'm going to grill the crap out of you every time you walk in the door, I'll let it go for now," Amber said as she moved over to Eeyore and patted his head. He looked at her with what seemed a thankful expression.

"Why thank you, Queen Amber," Patsy said with a bit of sarcasm and a lot of relief. She turned and moved down the hallway to her bedroom.

Eeyore waited impatiently at her door as she changed into her yoga pants and running shirt. She had some energy to burn and she wasn't going to do it by sitting in her apartment eating and drinking.

As she grabbed Eeyore's leash she decided a little buzz was exactly what the doctor had ordered for a nighttime run. There'd be no walking tonight if she wanted to sleep. She needed a good run instead, which Eeyore always put up with. If she got some side cramps at least she could focus on that instead of one very sexy neighbor.

It was all good. It would work for sure.

Eeyore looked at her as they moved down the staircase, preferring to start the workout early and avoid the elevators at the same time. She could swear she saw judgment in her dog's eyes.

"You don't know," she told him and his head tilted to the side. "Sure, he's sexy, but he's also arrogant and a pain in the ass. I'm much better off not knowing him."

Eeyore didn't talk back to her, so her sanity was clearly still in place, but she did feel slightly judged.

"I know. I know. I'm losing it a little," she told her dog. "But I'm also getting very little sleep and have a lot on my mind."

Eeyore whimpered a little as they neared the exit.

"A good run will do both of us good," she assured her dog. "And we'll wash all thoughts of the sexy doctor from our minds."

She was smiling as she moved across the street to the nearly empty park. She didn't worry about running at night—not with Eeyore at her side. She might know he was a big ball of fur, but he was big indeed and other people didn't know he was a gentle giant. No one had tried attacking her with him there.

She didn't have a dog for her protection. She had him because she loved him. But it was an added benefit. It was probably why Ryan had gifted the dog to her. She didn't mind though; she couldn't imagine not having him.

She began her run, and her worries faded away as she and Eeyore let off their steam from the day. Kyle was completely forgotten, she assured herself. Out of sight, out of mind.

It didn't take long for Patsy to get into a good rhythm, and Eeyore, used to their nightly strolls, whether walking or running, trotted easily beside her. When there was no one in the park, she'd undo his leash, knowing he wouldn't run from her—at least when there wasn't a group of hot men playing Frisbee.

Maybe she should rethink letting him off his leash. That incident had brought her nothing but trouble.

More people were in the park than usual at nine on a Thursday night. A sweet old couple were holding hands as they sat at a fountain, looking over and smiling at her and Eeyore as they passed, making Patsy's heart flutter at how charming it was.

A few teens were using the skate park to try out some flips, hooting and hollering before someone shushed them and they got kicked out. A few other runners passed her, and she gave them a nod, but she wasn't in the mood to visit with anyone.

She found her groove and it felt good. She was determined to think of anything other than Dr. Kyle Armistead. The more she ran, the surer she was she could do exactly that.

She looked ahead at the well-lit path and couldn't help but smile at the smooth muscles of the man in front of her. He definitely had runner's legs, which were currently flexing with each step he took.

The man didn't appear to be in a hurry as she wasn't running too fast, and she was gaining ground on him. Shadows cast along the path, but there were enough lights that she didn't feel isolated on this particular trail. It also gave her a muted view of the man about twenty yards ahead.

Not wanting to pass him, she matched her pace to his, allowing her eyes to soak in the smooth way he moved along the trail. She lost sight of him a few times as he turned corners but quickly caught up again.

She was happy to drool over the man. That meant she wasn't as infatuated with a certain doctor as she'd begun to think she was. That was certainly good news. She smiled at Eeyore, who was panting slightly as he kept pace with her.

But as she had thoughts of being attracted to another man, Patsy's thoughts went back to Kyle, to the way his scrubs fit him to perfection, to the way his dimpled cheek looked so adorable when he smiled, to the way she wanted to see him change in the locker room to see if he was as appealing naked as he was clothed.

The man she seemed to be unconsciously closing the gap on, reminded her of Kyle. That irritated her. Was she going to see Kyle in every stranger now? Was she going to make comparisons? At least the man was matching up and not coming up short, she thought with relief.

He disappeared again and Patsy picked up her pace a bit more—which turned out to be a mistake. Someone had left a water bottle on the path she didn't see, since her eyes had been searching for the man. Her foot tripped on it just as she began turning the corner—and she went down hard.

Eeyore instantly stopped and whimpered, licking her face as she cried out before silencing herself. She'd managed a twist at the last moment, but the side of her leg was throbbing, and she knew she'd scraped it pretty badly. It would've been worse if she'd been in shorts instead of running pants.

"This is gonna leave a bruise," she said to Eeyore. She was fighting tears. "It's okay. Maybe if I could get my mind out of the gutter, I wouldn't be such a klutz."

The dog seemed to nod in agreement. That made her glare at her favorite animal. He didn't seem offended.

"I guess you really do like falling at my feet."

Patsy tensed; she knew that voice all too well. She closed her eyes and took a deep breath before gaining the courage to look at the sexy legs she'd been staring at for the last ten minutes.

Of course the man running in front of her had reminded her of Kyle—it was him.

Slowly, her gaze traveled up his long legs, over his torso, and to his face. There was a smile there but a hint of worry in his eyes that made her heart thump.

Well crap!

This was just a perfect ending to a perfect day.

CHAPTER THIRTEEN

KYLE KNEW THE moment Patsy was behind him. She wasn't as quiet as she might believe she was, and her misnamed dog gave away even more. He enjoyed knowing she was there and had been running at far too slow a pace, hoping she'd catch up to him, wondering if she would.

It had been euphoric having her there, making all of his senses scream with the need to turn around and see her. If he'd slowed any more he would've been walking. But the anticipation of waiting for her to catch him had been more exhilarating than anything he'd felt in a long time.

He'd decided it was time to stop and wait for her when he'd heard her yelp. He'd instantly turned to find her on the ground, a water bottle on the path. He hadn't even noticed it, but must have skimmed over it with his long strides.

She didn't appear hurt, but he still felt a need to protect her. She tended to get a bit klutzy when she was nervous. Had she known he was ahead of her? Had it made her nervous? He could get used to the two of them running together. There was something healing about a night run, especially after a long day of surgery.

Eeyore looked at him with adoring eyes, so he kneeled down and scratched the dog's head. Eeyore sighed and eyed Kyle as if to ask why it had taken him so long to give a simple scratch. That made him smile.

He turned his attention back to Patsy who wasn't hero worshiping him like her dog was. That was slightly disappointing, but he was determined to change her mind about him. Something this intense between them shouldn't be ignored.

"It's you," she said between clenched teeth. "I should've known it was you."

Well that answered his question on whether or not she'd known it was him running in front of her. If she hadn't known, he wondered why she hadn't caught up to him or tried to pass. He'd been going at a snail's pace.

"Did you enjoy the view? You were behind me for quite a while," he said, his grin turning up when her cheeks flushed—and not from exertion. "I feel as if you're stalking me again."

Her mouth opened but no words came out. Instead she took in a breath, and he watched as she visibly tried composing herself. He wondered if it was a good or bad thing how much he flustered this woman.

"This is *my* park. I've been running here for two months," she pointed out. "Eeyore needs exercise at night."

"As I was the one in front . . ." He paused and flashed her his most wicked grin. "I'd say that answers who's stalking whom."

A myriad of emotions flashed across her face as she tried to compose a suitable response to him. It was fascinating to watch the varying expressions. She hypnotized him. He'd give every last dollar he had to know exactly what was happening in that big, beautiful brain of hers.

She was obviously attracted to him. There was no denying that, but for some reason she wasn't willing to act on it. He knew it wasn't because he was technically her boss. The hospital certainly didn't like romances blooming in their hallways, but it happened all the time and wasn't forbidden. No one was going to lose their job over it. Plus, both of them obviously knew how to keep it professional at work. It wasn't as if he'd take her right there on an OR table.

Though as soon as he had that thought, it was quite appealing. He wondered if he'd ever be able to look at another table again and not think of doing just that. Okay, maybe hospital romances weren't the smartest idea. But it didn't really matter because he was drawn to her. He'd tried avoiding her and that hadn't worked, so now something had to be done about it or he'd go insane.

"Most people normally run in the morning," she said when she came to some sort of conclusion in her mind. "So I wasn't expecting to see you here. I wasn't following you or anything. Okay, that sounds stupid. This is a big park. We can both run anytime we want to run." She stopped and huffed, and he could save her but he was having too much fun watching her grow more and more flustered.

"Of course you know you can run anytime you want. It's a public space. I'm just saying that we don't need to run into each other . . . or talk." She looked as if she was going to continue speaking, but she slammed her lips closed and glared at him as if she'd figured out she was rambling and he was enjoying her looking like a fool.

Her tongue darted out and licked her lips, and just like that all thoughts of teasing evaporated as his gaze zeroed in on the action. His body had been in a constant state of arousal from the minute she'd run into him. The problem had been growing more insistent the longer he didn't curb the craving.

His gaze drifted down her slender neck and over the curve of her breasts then were drawn to the hard peaks jutting against the tight fabric. Her breath hitched again and her nipples hardened a bit more.

She was responsive as hell from nothing more than a look. He couldn't imagine what she'd be like if he actually touched her. It was taking all his will power not to do just that. He could lift her, pull her into the bushes, and they could curb this hunger they were both feeling.

As if Eeyore could read his thoughts he let out a low bark, drawing Kyle's gaze away from Patsy's luscious breasts. Her eyes were slanted as she took shallow breaths. He wasn't sure what to say next. He was lost in a haze of lust. She finally gathered her thoughts together and sent him another withering look.

"You can stop dissecting my chest at any time. No one has done work on it," she said in a snotty voice.

He smiled before breaking out in laughter. It took a few moments before he was able to talk. "Oh, Patsy, you're a true joy," he said, feeling tears in the corners of his eyes. He hadn't laughed that hard in a while. "I wasn't thinking of plastic surgery right then. I was thinking of how much I want to see you naked for purely nonmedical reasons."

Their eyes were glued together, and she gasped at his bold words. He might as well be honest with her. He planned on having her in his bed, so it was better that she was aware of that. He hadn't ever enjoyed flirting. He loved sex, loved it a lot, but he'd never found it worth much effort to get. Not that he'd had to try too hard.

He could get lost in the depths of her eyes. They showed so much emotion. There was nothing at all fake about this woman, and he appreciated the true beauty of her. Normally he couldn't look at a person without thinking of what he wanted to change about them. That wasn't the case with Patsy. She was perfect just as she was.

"You can't say things like that," she whispered, her voice husky. "Or look at me like I'm your next meal."

"Maybe I'm hungry," he told her. There was no maybe about it.

Suddenly the fierceness of her gaze disappeared as she lifted a hand to her chest again. For a moment sadness flashed across her gaze. Then she pushed it away and scowled at him.

"Clothes are quite deceptive. I'm in no way perfect," she told him.

It took a few moments for her words to process in his muddled brain. What in the hell was she talking about?

"You look pretty perfect to me," he told her.

"I don't sleep with doctors—not ever, especially plastic surgeons who have unreal expectations of a female body."

He was more confused than ever.

"You're making no sense," he said. She glared.

"I have scars," she finally said, the words seeming to have been ripped from her.

"We all have scars," he told her. He could think of at least four on him right off the bat. The worst was when he'd fallen off the roof nearly giving his mother a heart attack and ending up in a leg cast for six weeks, which he'd thought was pretty awesome since he'd been smothered in attention.

He might be a plastic surgeon, but the beauty of his job was there was nothing he wasn't capable of fixing. That didn't mean everything needed to be fixed, though. As he looked at Patsy he realized again there wasn't a single thing about her he'd change. Not one.

"Mine's in a place that sucks," she told him with defiance.

"So what?" he said. He was utterly confused where this conversation was going.

"I don't get naked with people," she huffed. "I know you think this is going somewhere. I'll admit I find you attractive, but I'm not going to sleep with you, so you need to move on."

Her arms folded across her chest in a protective gesture. He couldn't stand not to touch her anymore. He reached out, and she flinched slightly as he cupped her cheek. She tried pulling away from him, but his fingers tightened. She was pulling away from him because she was afraid he'd find her ugly. That was unacceptable.

"You're stunning, Patsy. And something you might want to think about is the fact that looks aren't all that matter. There's so much more to you than a beautiful face and body. Your eyes shine with your thoughts, and the sound of your voice is enough to bring any man to his knees. I've wanted you from the moment I set eyes on you, and that feeling has only grown. If you honestly think I'd be turned off by a scar or ten scars, you should get to know me because I think I'm worth knowing, and I would never see anything wrong with someone I care about," he told her.

He was a little horrified at his honesty, but he didn't want to take the words back. He wasn't so foolish as to think he was in love with this woman after only knowing her for a few weeks, but he'd definitely say he couldn't get her off his mind—he had to know her better.

He had no doubt she was just as fascinated by him. What did the two of them have to lose in getting to know each other, possibly learning how to trust another person? Yes, Kyle trusted his family implicitly, but he'd never trusted a woman. He'd only seen them as having one purpose. Maybe he would've seen Patsy that way too had they fallen into bed together on that first day.

But since he'd been forced to chase her, he'd been watching her the entire time. If she disappeared from his life, he'd miss her, he'd hunt her down. He wasn't in any way ready to stop whatever it was that was happening between the two of them. And the longer this dance went on, the less it frightened him.

"You're making it really difficult for me to keep my distance from you," she admitted, and his euphoria soared within him.

Eeyore earned his name as he'd lost interest in the conversation and was napping right beside them, his head on his paws. Kyle was sure an earthquake could hit and the dog wouldn't stir.

He couldn't stand not to touch Patsy for a second longer, not when she was looking so vulnerable and lost. They were in the middle of a running trail where anyone could pass by, and he still didn't care.

Kyle normally kept public displays of affection to a minimum, preferring to not even kiss a woman in public, let alone touch her, but he didn't care around Patsy. He couldn't stand not having her in his arms any longer.

She let out a surprised gasp but didn't fight him as he sat down and pulled her legs over his, straddling her across his lap. She panted in his arms as he drew his lips closer to hers.

"This should've happened long ago," he told her.

With no more warning he closed the distance between them, gripped the back of her head, and locked his mouth with hers. She gasped at the zap of electricity between them, opening her lips for him to slide his tongue inside.

Heat exploded through him, and there was no hiding the evidence of how turned on he was as he pulled her more tightly against him, her legs straddled across his thighs. She felt exactly how he'd expected in his arms.

The heat was something he hadn't expected, though. He was on fire. As her tongue tentatively tangled with his, he knew he was on the verge of losing complete control. He never lost control—but with this woman he could fall to his knees if he wasn't careful.

She was everything he hadn't known he was looking for, and he felt as if he'd perish if she pushed him away. He was vaguely aware of where they were and of how heated their kiss was getting.

His hands traveled up and down her smooth back as she grew more comfortable with the kiss, her fingers sliding up his arms until they were tangled in his hair, her tongue growing greedier as their mouths crashed together in a symphony of pleasure.

He needed more. He wanted more. He *had* to have more!

He was losing control as he pulled her tightly to him. His hand shot down the curve of her ass, and he gripped her tight while pushing upward, rubbing his arousal against her hot core. It would be so easy to rip their clothes away and sink into pure heaven.

He began sliding his fingers into the top of her elastic waistband when they heard voices. His head was in a fog; it took several long seconds before he knew their little haven was about to be intruded upon. With an agonized moan, he pulled back and nearly came undone when Patsy whimpered her disapproval.

"We're about to have company," he told her.

Her glazed eyes looked at him, lust and satisfaction residing in their expressive depths. She trembled on his lap, and he thought again about dragging her into the bushes.

But as soon as he had the thought, two runners passed them, whistling before going by. They were alone again. He thought about resuming where they'd left off, but as he turned back to Patsy he saw a different awareness flash into her eyes.

She was horrified. She scrambled from his lap, and he let her. She was definitely on shaky knees as she stood, but his weren't much steadier.

Eeyore looked up with bored eyes as if deciding if he wanted to rise at all.

"Come on, Eeyore, it's time to go home," Patsy said in a trembling voice.

"We can talk more at my place," he offered.

She looked at him with horror.

"Um . . . no. I think that's as much talking as I can handle for the night," she told him.

He smiled at her. Though his body was on fire, he didn't regret a single moment of the night. It had been perfect. He definitely needed a cold shower, but that was worth the kiss.

Patsy had a fire raging inside of her, and she needed the right man to set it free to burn as wildly as it wanted to. He was more than willing to step up to the job.

"I . . . um . . . I better get back. I'll see you at work . . . later," she said, her words halting in her muddled brain.

"I'll walk with you," he told her.

"I'm good on my own. Finish your run," she said.

"Not a chance, Patsy," he told her.

She huffed, but she didn't argue as they slowly made their way back to the apartment building. He didn't want their time together to end. But even if they went their separate ways tonight, he knew they were just beginning.

That would be how he got through the night. That would be how he could be patient. She'd be his . . . and it wouldn't be that much longer.

CHAPTER FOURTEEN

THE TAP, TAP, tapping wouldn't leave her dream. Patsy twisted in her bed, but still the knocking persisted. Finally, her eyes opened and she looked over at her clock and groaned. It was four AM, and she hadn't gotten to sleep until at least two.

Her roommate was gone, and she had no other choice but to get up when she finally figured out the knocking wasn't in her dream but at her front door. Who in the world would be so rude as to knock on her door in the middle of the night?

She should've checked, but fury was making her reckless. She threw open the door, not caring that she was in a short nighty and her hair was all over the place. She blinked several times when she realized it was Kyle, looking far too good for the middle of the night.

He didn't say a word as he took his time looking at her from the souls of her feet to the top of her hair and back down again. Her eyes narrowed even more.

"What in the world do you need at this hour?" she asked, hating how her body warmed at his approving gaze.

"I want you," he told her in a low voice that had her stomach trembling, her nipples tightening, and her body turning molten hot. She opened her mouth like a fish out of water, but no words escaped.

He smiled slow and easy, and she was tempted to grab the front of his shirt and drag him inside her place. This man was far too dangerous to be living so close to her. She might be able to resist him at the hospital, just barely, but if he kept showing up at her apartment in the middle of the night she was a goner.

"As much as I want to pursue the invitation in your eyes, that has to come later," he told her, making her even more confused. "We've been called into the hospital."

"What?" She couldn't keep up with him. She hadn't gotten much sleep, she excused in her own head.

"There's a patient, and I've been called in. You want to learn, right?" he asked.

"Yes, yes, of course," she said, coming fully awake. This was about her job. Her job mattered to her.

"All right. As delicious as you look as you are, you might want to put on more clothes," he told her when she didn't move.

Patsy didn't say anything, just turned and walked away from him, leaving her door open as she moved to her bedroom. It took a few more seconds to clear her head before she grabbed her scrubs and went to the bathroom and threw her hair on top of her head, took a one-minute shower, then dressed. She was back in the living room in under ten minutes.

Kyle didn't say anything as he walked out of the apartment beside her, waited while she locked it up, then placed his hand on the small of her back as they quickly moved down the staircase.

Being next to him was confusing Patsy in a way she didn't remember feeling before. It seemed everything about this man caused unwanted emotions to filter through her. She hated it, yet strove for it at the same time. It was completely odd for her, some- one who'd always had it so together.

Kyle led her to his car and the moment they were locked in- side she thought it might have been wiser to take a cab. His scent was intoxicating, and the more she was around this man, the more she realized she was going to do something she'd regret.

She tried to move as close to the door as possible, and he turned and looked at her with a wink and a smile as if he could read her mind. She stared back at him, defiance in her eyes.

But her frustration drained at the raw desire in his expression. She couldn't remember a man ever looking at her like that before. Yes, men hit on her, and yes, she'd flirted before. But this couldn't be called harmless flirting.

This was raw and so intensely real she couldn't explain it. Why was she fighting it? Maybe because she was a fool, or maybe she'd remember all the reasons later. But either way, she wouldn't be so dang confused anymore.

It wasn't a long drive to the hospital, but she was a total mess by the time they arrived. Neither of them had spoken the entire time. The second she stepped into those sterile walls, she cast aside her worries. There was a patient and they always came first.

As if Kyle felt the same about the hospital as she did, his demeanor changed as well. He was professional as he told her to scrub up and meet him in the OR. Patsy went into the changing room and suited up then met Kyle in the scrub room where they stood side by side, taking their time cleaning up for the surgery.

This was mechanical. It calmed her. This was exactly what she needed, even if she was right next to the man who'd rocked her world only a few short hours before.

Nope. She pushed that train of thought right out of her head as soon as she had it.

"Are you ready to shine?" Kyle asked as he held up his hands.

"Or fail. You might have picked the wrong person," she warned him.

He smiled at her, his expression full of confidence. This was why he was such a sought after surgeon. This was why he could go anywhere he wanted. He knew what to do, and he knew he was the best at it.

"I don't ever choose wrong," he said. She had no doubt there was a double meaning to his words. A shudder wracked through her as she followed him into the operating room.

She was either going to shine today or fall on her ass. And Patsy didn't like to fail, so option two wasn't acceptable. She'd show them what she had. A confident smile filled her expression.

She was where she loved to be, and she was with the person she wanted to be with, whether she admitted it or not.

CHAPTER FIFTEEN

KYLE MIGHT BE putting on a hell of a face but that kiss with Patsy had done things to him he hadn't known could be done. She was so damn beautiful, but there was so much more to her than that.

She'd intrigued him from the moment he'd met her in the park, and his desire for her had only grown over time. The two of them were heading toward an inevitable conclusion, and for once in his life Kyle didn't want to run from it.

As he waited by the table, he took a moment to study the way she walked with confidence, the way her eyes took in everything about their patient. She was going to make a hell of a doctor, and that was only one part of her. The longer this went on, the more he was going to lose himself in her. Kyle didn't realize he was so completely absorbed in her until his scrub nurse's words came through his muddied brain.

"Is everything okay?" she asked.

Kyle shook the cobwebs from his brain. This was no place to get lost. He had to be one hundred percent on his game in this room. It was unacceptable to be anything other than that. In this room he didn't matter—only his patient did.

No everything wasn't okay. But he assured himself he'd make it that way soon. He'd get over his utter absorption with the woman once he bedded her. He knew once would never be enough, but at least his hormones would be tamed enough to think of other things besides her twenty-four/seven.

Or so he hoped.

"I'm good. Let's get started," Kyle told the nurse who nodded but seemed a bit unsure. Kyle really needed to pull it together before the staff started talking.

Patsy moved across from him and looked eager, her own turbulent thoughts cast aside as she also became a professional.

"Where do you want me?" she asked.

He took a calming breath at her choice of words. His body wasn't in the best of shape right now and that was dangerous. He had to push thoughts of exactly where he wanted her from his head.

"Right where you are," he told her. "Let's begin."

Two hours into the surgery Kyle's desire was certainly tamed as his admiration for Patsy increased. He hadn't performed a surgery with her yet, and that was a shame. She was talented, with an eye for detail, and a demeanor that made other staff members give her their respect and admiration.

Her hands were steady, and her voice was calm. She didn't have too much pride to ask questions, but she had the knowledge and skill to not need to do it too often. She was going to excel at her job the longer she did it, and he was proud to be one of her teachers, proud to have her across an operating table from him.

When all that was left were some final stitches, Kyle stepped back from the table. "Are you okay to finish, Dr. Lander?"

She didn't look away from their patient as her steady hand inserted another stitch. "Yes, thank you," she said. Her lips turned up.

Only an attending surgeon confident in his resident would leave them on their own, even at this stage in the procedure. They both knew that, and she was proud of herself. He was glad to be a part of helping her grow.

"Good. I'll talk to you when you're finished," he said as he moved away, taking off his gloves and gown as he left the room.

Kyle showered and changed then did his paperwork quickly before heading to the lobby to wait for her. He knew Patsy would try to sneak away and talk to him later. It was nearly noon and both of them had been up for close to two days straight with minimal rest. But they were going to the same place, and he hoped the same bed.

Just as he'd thought, he saw her walking toward the exit doors, glancing behind her as if she carried a victory of getting away from him. He smiled from his place near a large column. He waited until she was exiting the door to step beside her.

"Ready to go home?" he asked.

She whipped around to see him, her eyes wide, her luscious lips parted. Damn she was a beautiful woman, especially with flushed cheeks and sleepy eyes.

"I wasn't expecting a ride home," she told him. He could see the wheels turning in her head to see how she could get out of getting back into a vehicle with him. He wasn't having it.

"Of course I'll take you home. I brought you here," he told her.

Just as he had when they'd left the apartment, he placed his hand on her back and led her to his car. He felt a slight shudder pass through her, and his body, which had calmed during surgery, instantly hardened again. He wanted this woman, and knowing she wanted him too made him even hungrier.

They began the drive home, both of them tired, but not in a sleepy kind of way. Sleep wouldn't come easy to either of them with the way their bodies stirred. It was because of both the surgery and their desire. They'd had a successful procedure, now they needed to have a romp in his bed, and then they'd both sleep like babies. Scratch that, babies didn't sleep at all. They'd sleep like exhausted puppies.

They were pulling into the apartment complex when her stomach let out a loud growl that had him laughing and her cheeks flushing. He now had an excuse to get her into his place.

"Come on, Dr. Lander. I dragged you out in the middle of the night; the least I can do is feed you," he told her as he led her to the elevator.

"I'm fine. I just want to take a nap," she told him, moving to push the button for her floor.

He blocked her. "No way. I'd feel far too guilty sending you off with your stomach screaming its displeasure at being empty for too long," he said. "Besides we can go over the case notes." He knew that would get her to his place.

She sighed and nodded. "I guess it's better to go over that now rather than later."

They made it to his floor, and he found himself slightly nervous at having her come into his place. It was still a mess as he hadn't been there very long, but at least he had leftovers that he only had to warm.

Kyle could certainly cook. He'd learned how to do it so he didn't have to eat out all the time, but with his busy schedule he found he cooked less and less. Besides, it wasn't exactly fun to make a meal for one all the time.

Being alone was something Kyle had always assumed he wanted-ed. He *had* always wanted that. Until one dark-haired woman had stepped into his life.

"I'll get the food ready. You pour some wine and sit down," he told her as he pulled out a bottle from the fridge.

Patsy looked at her watch and frowned. "It's barely one in the afternoon," she told him.

"That's only what the clocks say. We haven't slept, so it's nighttime for us," he argued.

She laughed as she took his electric wine opener and removed the cork then poured two glasses while he heated spaghetti and added extra cheese on top.

"Let's sit on the couch. I've had enough hard seats for the day," he told her as he carried both their plates to his living room.

Patsy followed him and wedged herself into the corner of his couch before accepting the plate he was holding out. She set her wine glass on the coffee table in front of her, putting some distance between them. He always had enjoyed a challenge.

"We haven't had a chance to talk much," he told her as he took his first bite of food. The taste awoke his hunger and he had to keep himself from devouring the entire plate in a few bites.

"We talk every day," she told him. Then she made his body ache as she sighed and licked her lips. "This is fantastic." Her hunger went into overdrive like his as she stopped speaking and concentrated on eating.

He didn't answer for a bit. "There's a great Italian place down the road I order from at least twice a week," he told her.

"I want the name. I don't think I've found it yet," she said. Her plate was halfway finished.

"I'll take you there tonight after you get some sleep," he suggested.

She laughed. "I shouldn't eat pasta twice in one day." She spoke the words, but he could see she wanted more. Her food was nearly gone, and she looked as if she could finish an entire second plate.

"You can eat it three times a day if you want. You don't have enough meat on your bones for it to make a difference."

She laughed. "It depends on the week," she assured him. "Weeks like this when I barely get a chance to eat everything seems to shrink, but then I have a couple of rare days off and I do nothing but stuff my face and my clothes get too tight."

"Mama Calzones has the best tiramisu I've ever eaten," he said, really wanting to take her out for dinner. And not buying for one second that she had the ability to put on extra weight. She was far too active.

Her eyes lit up as she finished the last of her spaghetti and rose to take her plate to the kitchen.

"That's just mean. That's my favorite desert," she told him over her shoulder.

He finished his own food and set his plate on the coffee table as she returned and picked up her wine.

"Then it's a date," he said.

She licked her lips again and tasted her wine, and his pants grew painfully tight as he swelled. She couldn't do anything without him wanting her, but sitting in his house on his couch with her lips wet from wine and her eyes sparkling with humor . . . he was a slave at her feet.

"It's friends getting dinner," she countered as she finished her wine then looked at the glass with a frown as if it didn't dare be empty. He fought a smile and grabbed the bottle and refilled both their glasses.

"We're much more than friends, Patsy," he told her, sitting closer to her after the wine was poured.

He heard her breath hitch at his words. He reached out and ran a finger across the bottom of her lip as moisture from the wine dripped a little. He wanted to mop it up with his tongue, then pour the rest of the bottle of wine all over her body and lick that up as well.

"We don't really know each other so we aren't anything," she said, her voice husky.

"I want to change that," he told her, pausing as he shifted a little closer. "I want to change it right now."

He was done with his wine. He didn't need it to get drunk, not when he had her in front of him. She'd been making his head spin for weeks.

"It's not a good idea," Patsy said, but he heard her desire, felt the tremor in her body.

"If you're leaving, you better do it now . . . or we're going to my bedroom," he warned. He leaned down and ran his lips across her neck and into the soft hollow at her shoulder, gently nipping her skin.

Her breathing deepened as she set aside her glass and reached for his head, running her fingers in his hair as her head fell back, giving him more access.

"I don't think I can leave," she said, just the slightest trace of frustration in her tone.

As much as it pained him to do so, he pulled back, looking in her eyes. His desire was calling him every foolish name in the book, but he didn't want her to say their first time was coerced by him. He wanted her as accountable as he was.

"I want you so bad; I've ached for weeks," he said. "I need you to want me just as much."

She looked at him confused as if she wanted him to make the decision for her. He wanted to do that too, but he couldn't. Not this time. The next kiss would come from her or it wasn't going to happen. He waited, calling himself every inventive name he'd ever thought of in his entire lifetime.

Emotions flickered across her face as she struggled over what to do. He wasn't sure if he'd survive if she walked out his door. He'd never respected a woman this much, never cared so much if she wanted him or not. Of course, on that note, he couldn't remember a woman not wanting him, especially one he desired.

Her gaze dropped to his mouth, and he groaned. She licked her lips as she leaned forward the slightest bit. She was finally shutting down her highly intelligent brain and allowing her body to take over.

She closed her eyes and closed the gap between them, her lips tasting his. That's all the incentive he needed. He pulled her onto his lap and took over the kiss, losing himself in her softness.

She moaned into his mouth, and this time they weren't in a public park or a hospital corridor. This time there was a bed close by, and he planned on taking full advantage of it.

She shuddered against him as he broke from her lips and kissed his way across her cheek, circling the lobe of her ear while his hand traveled over her back and to her side, his fingers brushing the side of her breast.

She pushed into him, her hips pressing forward as her breasts rubbed against his chest. He wanted their clothes gone, but he also didn't want to rush this. The sensation was too good, the anticipation too great.

She arched her neck, and he kissed his way up her throat, tasting vanilla and cinnamon, making him so damn hungry for more. He moved upward, needing her lips again. His hands moved to her hips, and he pulled her against him, making sure she knew how turned on he was, how turned on she'd made him.

She cried out against his lips as her tongue danced with his. She reached up and gripped his hair tightly in her fingers, yanking him closer.

In one smooth motion, he moved his hands to her luscious butt and rose. Her legs wrapped around him, and their kiss didn't end as he moved toward his bedroom, praying he didn't trip on one of the boxes scattered throughout the apartment. He pulled from her mouth so he could see, and she buried her face in his neck. He groaned as her teeth nipped at his skin before her tongue soothed the spot.

Somehow they made it to the bedroom. He wasn't quite sure how since his vision blurred with her wicked little mouth doing the most beautiful things to his neck and jaw. The two of them fell onto the bed, her soft body pressed beneath his.

He sank his hips against hers, and her legs wrapped tightly around him. If there weren't clothes between them, he'd be sunk deep within her hot folds right then.

"I need you so damn bad," he growled before kissing her deep and hard until neither of them were breathing right. When he pulled away and looked at her swollen lips, he felt like a caveman who'd marked his woman.

"Take me. Please," she said, pushing her hips up and rubbing against him.

He didn't need to be asked twice. The next minute was filled with him ripping off their clothes as his fingers shook with each new revelation of skin. She was as perfect as he'd always pictured she'd be. More so, even.

He needed to touch her everywhere, taste each new piece of her skin, and make her come again and again. He'd never get enough of her, never. She was his now, and he needed to brand her.

He barely pulled away from her long enough to reach into his nightstand to get the condom he almost forgot to put on. That wasn't like him, not at all. Protection was always the first thing on his mind when he was with a woman. But Patsy did something to him no other woman had. She made him stop thinking.

Finally he was sheathed, his body poised over hers. And then he paused. His breath was taken away with the beauty of her, with the magic of this moment. He'd desired her for so long, but this was more than sex. This was so much more.

"Open your eyes, Patsy," he said, not recognizing his own voice. It was filled with wonder and need.

Her eyes cracked open as if it hurt her to do so. There was need and desire and awe in her expression. It made him feel powerful, and wanted, and he knew he was right where he was supposed to be.

Only when he gazed deeply in her eyes, did he finally push forward, slow and steady, groaning at the ecstasy of sinking into her folds. Her body cradled him tight all the way down his length until he was fully buried within her.

"So good," he said in reverence.

"Oh, yes," she replied as her arms circled his back and her nails dug into his skin.

He began to move; long, slow thrusts in and out of her body. They gazed at each other, the most intimate moment he'd ever experienced. But soon, it was too much. The pleasure grew as they searched for that ultimate moment.

He sped up, moving faster, his body rocking against hers as her hands climbed up and down his back. Their bodies grew damp with pleasure and exertion, and then she tightened around him, squeezing him as she let out a cry and came.

He sank deep and his own pleasure spilled from him, his body shaking for how incredibly good it felt. She kept her arms wrapped tightly around him as small shudders continued passing through her body.

It took a long while for their breathing to calm. Only then did he find the energy to roll over. But he couldn't let her go. This was new for him as well. He'd never needed to hold on to a woman after sex.

He cradled her to him as his hand rubbed against the smooth skin of her back. He was almost frightened at how intimate this moment was, but he wasn't scared enough to let her go. He *couldn't* let her go. His fingers gently moved over her scar, letting her know without words how beautiful he found her.

Neither of them spoke. Kyle realized she had to be just as frightened as he was at how intimate this had become.

He'd had sex with many women, but he'd never felt whatever it was he was feeling then. It should make him want to get up and run. But it didn't. Instead, he let it all go, shut down his mind, and closed his eyes.

He was right where he was supposed to be. And he wasn't letting her get away from him.

CHAPTER SIXTEEN

I**T WAS PITCH** black in the room when Patsy woke up with a start, panic filling her as she realized she didn't know where she was. There was something holding her down and she opened her mouth, ready to scream.

Kyle mumbled beside her as he shifted, and the day came flooding back to her. All of it. Him at her door in the middle of the night, the ride to and from the hospital, the surgery, the dinner, the . . . sex.

The best sex.

The most intimate sex.

The life changing sex.

Now she got it!

Patsy stilled as her body hummed with a new need Kyle had awakened in her. He'd given her so much pleasure what had to have only been hours before. And then she'd fallen asleep in his arms, completely comfortable, completely safe.

And she wanted more.

She couldn't ever remember wanting more. Sex had never been like that for her. It had never been so intense, so beautiful, so perfect. She'd never felt as if she was right where she belonged. She hadn't even thought about her scar. She hadn't been self-conscious of it, not even when he'd traced it. He'd made her feel that damn good.

That thought scared the hell out of her. She had plans and dreams and they didn't include a man—at least not yet.

She couldn't be like all those girls who went all gaga over a man and forgot about her own dreams. She wouldn't do that to herself. She wouldn't fall in love. Yes, she'd seen examples of true love and the beauty of it. But she'd also seen the devastation that only supposed love could bring.

As she listened to Kyle breathing deeply beside her she realized she was in serious danger of doing just that with this particular man. She'd be such a fool if she did. She tried comforting herself; people had sex all the time. Co-workers had sex more often than bunnies. It didn't have to change anything. They could go right back to where they'd been before the sex. Or they could go back to before that—when they didn't know each other.

The thought of doing that horrified her. She wasn't sure she could pass him in the hallway remembering what it was like having him buried so deep inside her she didn't know where she began and he ended. She was dang sure she wouldn't want to see him pressed up against another woman in some dark corridor.

She was in trouble.

She turned her head and saw it was ten. They'd slept the entire day away. Of course neither of them had slept much, and she normally went weeks with little rest. But still, she couldn't remember the last time she'd even slept six hours, let alone eight.

Because Patsy wanted to do nothing more than lie in the safety of Kyle's arms, she forced herself to move. She was already too comfortable in his bed, and that was unsafe for many reasons.

First, she had plans that didn't include Kyle. And second, she knew who he was. He was a playboy through and through. So even if she could let down her guard and fall for him, he'd be victorious in his conquest and be done with her. And then she'd be embarrassed at work and heartbroken. That was a lose-lose situation she wanted nothing to do with.

It took her a good five minutes to inch her way from beneath his heavy arm and leg. She stood over the bed, her eyes adjusting to the dark. Their dinner plans had definitely flown out the window. That was good. She wanted to try the Italian place, and if she'd gone there with him she was afraid she'd never be able to go back again.

She was getting too sentimental, too weepy, and they'd only slept together one time. She had a real problem she refused to deal with.

Turning away from the sight of his beautifully naked body, Patsy forced herself to walk away. She gathered her scattered clothes, hoping she didn't forget anything, then went to the bathroom where she discovered her panties were missing.

There was no way she was going to find them in the dark without making noise. Mortified at leaving them behind, but left with no other choice, she made her way from his apartment, praying no one she knew saw her walk of shame.

Not daring to use the elevator she took the stairs to her floor and let herself into her apartment, instant guilt filling her at the sight of her dog gazing up at her with accusing eyes.

"I'm so sorry," she told Eeyore who instantly forgave her, rushing up to her and giving her a quick lick on the cheek as she knelt to pet him.

"He's just fine. He was pouty long enough that I took him for a walk to Antonio's and he got his own slice of peperoni pizza," Amber said from where she was leaning against the wall. "It looks like you weren't at work this whole time."

Her friend took in her disheveled appearance and flushed face, making Patsy blush more deeply.

"Um, well, Kyle picked me up for an emergency surgery, and then we were hungry . . . and well, um . . ." Her voice trailed off. She felt like a school child being interrogated.

Amber laughed.

"I know exactly what that um means, and it's about time. You're wound too tightly; you need a good roll in the sack more than anyone I know," Amber told her.

"I shouldn't have forgotten my dog," Patsy said as she petted the grateful animal.

"Eeyore is far from abused," Amber said. "And you can go back to bed even though it's obvious you just came from one. He's been walked and fed."

"I shouldn't be tired at all. I slept forever," Patsy said with a yawn. But she was tired. She felt as if she hadn't slept in a year, and muscles were sore that she hadn't known could get sore.

Amber laughed again. "Sex wears a person out. I miss being that tired." With that her friend went down the hallway, leaving Patsy with her dog.

"Want to go to bed?" she asked him.

She would swear Eeyore smiled. He definitely understood her. That was without question. He led the way to her bedroom and Patsy grabbed her jammies and went into the bathroom where she took a long, hot shower, trying to relieve some of the aches in her body.

Some of the soreness evaporated, but the empty feeling of not having Kyle sunk deep within her was an ache she couldn't take care of. She figured there was no way she'd go back to sleep, but as she crawled beneath her covers with Eeyore at the foot of her bed keeping her feet warm, she closed her eyes and was out instantly.

Maybe tomorrow she'd feel like herself again.

Or maybe not.

CHAPTER SEVENTEEN

KYLE JERKED UP in bed as his head twisted from side to side. Fight or flight kicked in as he pushed away grogginess. All of this occurred in about two seconds, but just that quickly, he calmed himself down as he realized what had woken him.

On his nightstand, his pager was buzzing, a noise so ingrained he was instantly awake. Rubbing a hand over his face, he was shocked by the amount of stubble there. He turned and looked at his clock, seeing it was two in the morning.

What the hell?

He ran his hand across his cold bedsheets and realized Patsy had been gone a long time, though her scent hung heavy in the room. Not only had he slept like the dead, something he hadn't done in at least ten years, probably longer, but he didn't know what to think about the fact that Patsy had snuck off like some hooker he'd picked up on the street corner.

He should be relieved.

He wasn't.

Looking at his pager, he picked up his cell and sent a message letting them know he'd be there ASAP. Then he rose and stretched, his body sore from his incredible activity with Patsy then sleeping like the damn dead.

There was no emergency at the hospital, so he took his time in the shower, letting the hot water soothe his aching body. He guaranteed he wouldn't sleep like that again for the next ten years. He was a doctor. Sleep was a luxury.

All through the shower he told himself he was glad she'd left. He hated messy morning afters. Ninety percent of the women he'd been with were aware he wasn't a relationship guy, but there were the ten percent who wanted more. Those were the cases where he immediately regretted having sex. The pleasure wasn't enough to deal with the drama.

But he'd enjoyed falling asleep with Patsy in his arms. And he didn't like that she'd snuck away from his place. Stepping into his bedroom, he went to his walk-in closet and grabbed some clothes, not caring what he wore.

When he stepped back into the bedroom a piece of red caught the corner of his eye and he bent down, his lips turning up in a smile, his body going instantly rock hard.

She'd forgotten her panties.

He lifted the lacy things, fascinated with their sexiness. Patsy was so damn conservative on the outside, but she was passionate in the bedroom. He'd opened her up less than twelve hours earlier and wasn't ready to let go. He stuffed the panties in his pocket.

He hurried to get to the hospital. He knew she'd be there.

Though Patsy had indeed left his bed without a goodbye, Kyle smiled as he made his way to work. He was going to see her again and couldn't wait to touch her, make her blush, possibly even get her in an on-call room where he could test if the sex was as mind-boggling good when they were fully wake. They'd both been tired the day before. That could've heightened the sex, he tried to reason with himself.

Or he was a fool and trying to justify his fascination with one certain woman.

He arrived in the OR wing of the hospital just as Patsy turned a corner. She was looking down and he stopped, enjoying the view of her long legs as she drew closer. He could still taste her skin on his tongue.

The second she looked up, she tripped, then righted herself. She gave a curt nod and planned on walking by. Kyle's good mood evaporated instantly. She masked her beautiful features, but he'd seen that face filled with passion. There was no way he was allowing her to treat him like some hospital booty call.

She might be back to her cool self with her hair pulled tightly back, minimal makeup, and bland expression, but he knew the real Patsy, or was beginning to. He wanted to delve a hell of a lot deeper.

"Good morning," he said, his voice deep, seductive. He wrapped his fingers around her arm to stop her from running.

Her cheeks flushed. "I don't have time to chat," she said. "I'm late." She tried pulling from his grasp without making it seem like a struggle. People passed by them.

"You have a second," he said, and she stiffened.

"Let's not make this awkward," she told him.

He smiled, waiting for her to look him in the eyes again. It didn't take long because he knew she wouldn't want any passersby's to see his hand on her arm. He was a proper distance from her body, but people would talk—her worst nightmare.

"You forgot something at my place," he said, letting go and reaching into his pocket, pulling out the red scrap of lace. He kept them in his fist so no one would have a clue what he was holding.

He didn't think it was possible for someone's face to turn that shade of red. It made him want to push her into the nearest empty room and see exactly how heated he could make her.

She reached out to snag them, but he stuffed them back in his pocket. "I think I'll hold on to them since you snuck out in the middle of the night. You'll know where to find me to get them back." She huffed and looked at him like he was a crazy person. He didn't break eye contact.

Without another word she stormed off, her stride long and angry. Kyle's good mood returned. If she didn't care about him or what had happened between them, there was no way she'd react the way she did.

She was fighting her feelings for him as much as he normally fought any kind of commitment. Maybe he was a goner with this woman. That would certainly be a first.

"Dr. Armistead?" a voice called, pulling Kyle from his thoughts as he turned to find his favorite nurse standing in a doorway.

"Hi Helen," he replied. "Sorry I'm late."

"Technically you're early," she said with a smile. "But thanks for coming in. I'm concerned about your patient from three days ago, and you were due in at six this morning anyway."

Helen didn't overreact and didn't misjudge situations. If she was worried, there was a reason for her to be.

"Take me to her and explain the problem on the way," he told her.

Patsy would continue to stay on his mind, but he could compartmentalize for his patients. When they came to him he promised to take care of them and that's exactly what he was going to do.

"Rita's skin graft on her left cheek doesn't seem to be taking. I'm worried about an infection and want you to see right away since it's her face," Helen said. "She's been trying not to complain, but she's also been in pain, unable to sleep and not wanting to take meds. I convinced her to have a dose a couple of hours ago."

The two of them walked to the patient's room together and Kyle put thoughts of Patsy aside. He'd do his job, and when things slowed down he'd find his girl.

They were nowhere close to being over. She could run but there wasn't anywhere she could hide, not in his domain. Let the chase begin.

CHAPTER EIGHTEEN

PATSY HAD ALWAYS followed one rule—do not sleep with co-workers. There was a specific reason for that rule—moments like the one she'd just encountered. Morning afters were horrific, or so she'd been told. She was very aware how true that was after seeing Kyle in the sacred halls of her hospital.

How long would it take to not be mortified at the sight of him? Looking at him had reminded her of everything they'd done together, and it wasn't an unpleasant memory. But knowing she'd never be doing it with him again made seeing him painful. She had never imagined sex could be so amazing.

None of that mattered though. She had to pull herself together, and fast. She was meeting Nicole for lunch, the master interrogator. There'd be no way to hide how she felt about Kyle if her sister caught so much as a whiff of this.

Maybe she could file the memories away and pretend it never happened. That thought was less than appealing, especially when she had long, lonely nights ahead of her. Her lifestyle was her choice. No one had forced it on her. But on the rare occasion she let her guard down, she admitted it was lonely at times.

She quickly made her way to the café where Nic was meeting her. Sitting down, she pulled her compact from her purse and groaned at her image. She might convince her sister she looked like this because of a hard day's work, but if she was honest she'd say she looked like she'd been thoroughly pleasured for many, many hours. Her lips were swollen, her neck reddened, and, although her sis couldn't see underneath the clothes, her body was satisfyingly sore with some definite sex marks on her skin.

She'd never hide this from Nicole, but she would give it a valiant effort.

Just looking at herself caused flashes of the night before to run through her muddled brain, of how he'd climbed on top of her, of how his lips had tasted every inch of her skin, of how that pleasure had built . . . and built . . . and . . .

Stop it!

She internally screamed at herself as she dumped cold water on a napkin and held it against her forehead. She was seriously in bad shape, and no matter how she tried talking herself down, telling herself to forget, she couldn't pull it together as easily as she normally did.

"Is something wrong, my darling sister?"

Crap! Of course Nic was right on time. No traffic jam would stop her sister from finding her in a mess, mumbling to herself as she tried to cool her fevered body.

"I'm good," Patsy said as she attempted a nonchalant smile. Nic looked perfect as usual in a green blouse and slim fitting slacks that molded to her perfect frame. Even childbirth hadn't lessened her sister's beauty. Hell, it had enhanced her already perfect curves.

Nic sat across from her with an inquisitive look on her face. Patsy knew that look well, knew her sister was analyzing the situation and would have it summed up in no time at all. Dang it. She should've stated an emergency and cancelled this lunch.

Before Nic could say anything, the waitress came and took their order. With the café close to the hospital, the wait staff knew how to feed people fast so they could eat and get back to work, one advantage in Patsy's corner.

Alone again, Patsy reluctantly looked at her sister, who was beginning to smile as light dawned in her knowing eyes.

"Are those signs of sex I see on your neck?" Nic asked, her lips turning up in a megawatt smile.

Kyle had gotten a bit . . . frisky as he'd tasted her. Makeup didn't seem to be covering the evidence of his excitement. She should've worn a damn turtleneck beneath her scrubs.

"No. I have a rash," Patsy said, her cheeks flushing. She never had been a good liar. It wasn't a good trait in her field of work; she couldn't assure a family everything was okay when it wasn't.

"I don't think I've ever seen a hickey on you," Nic said in wonder. "Not *ever*. Not even as a teen. It had to have taken a lot of skill for some guy to mark you."

"No one has marked me," Patsy said with a glare as her fingers traced her neck where Kyle's mark beamed out like a damn lighthouse beacon.

"I want details. A *lot* of details," Nic said as the waitress dropped off their food. Patsy picked up a few fries and stuffed them in her mouth so she had an excuse not to talk. "I'm patient. Take your time eating."

Patsy was trying to form a feasible story in her muddled brain. But sex must have made her IQ drop because she was coming up blank.

"Waiting," Nicole patiently said, taking delicate nips from her onion rings. Her sister looked elegant even while eating cheap diner food.

"I didn't plan on sleeping with him," Patsy finally said. The truth might actually set her free if that saying meant anything.

"I get it. Been there, done that," Nic said with a laugh. "Who is it? How was it?"

"I don't want to talk about it," Patsy told her.

"Because it was terrible?" Nic questioned.

"I wish," Patsy said with a sigh. She was giving in. Of course she was. "It was the best night of my life, but it can't happen again."

"Why not? You're an adult. I'm assuming he's of legal age," Nic said with a laugh.

"I'm glad you're amused by my misery," Patsy said with another glare.

"I'm never amused by anyone's unhappiness," Nic said. "But clearly you aren't miserable. You're just confused."

"More than confused. I don't have time for an affair, and if I did it wouldn't be with an arrogant doctor who changes bed partners more often than he changes his sheets."

"Did he say he didn't want to see you again?" Nic asked, her eyes narrowing.

"No," Patsy admitted. "But I know."

"How do you know?" Nic asked.

"Because I've been around this type of man since I began school. They like to wrack up the notches on their bedposts. It's just who they are."

"Maybe you should talk to him. Most fights we have with other people are one-sided," Nic pointed out.

"We aren't exactly in a fight. I snuck off when he was asleep, and now I'm avoiding him. I have a career to think about."

"Honey, you're a great doctor and will only grow better over time, but don't let your personal life go to hell because of it. There's more to life than work," Nic said.

"I don't want more right now," Pasty told her.

"You know you could always bring him to the house for dinner," Nic said, clearly excited at the prospect.

"There's not a chance of that happening," Patsy told her.

"Oh, come on. That's a clear way of judging if he's strong enough to last. You know how the boys are."

Nicole wasn't kidding. Not a single guy Patsy had shown an interest in had lasted past one visit with her in-laws. Her sister's husband and his cousins were incredibly over-protective of Patsy, especially since she'd almost died as a teenager. They didn't think any man was good enough for her.

Maybe that would be the best way to get rid of Kyle. He'd take one look at her family and run for the hills. The thought was oddly depressing. But she shook her head as she tried convincing herself that's what she wanted.

"He won't want to come, even if I invite him," Patsy said.

"You won't know unless you try," Nic told her.

Before Patsy could respond her pager went off. She looked at the message gratefully as she stuffed the last bite of her burger in her mouth and stood.

"I have to run," she said.

"Saved by the ding," Nic told her with a laugh.

Patsy rolled her eyes as she stood. Nic joined her and gave her a big hug before letting Patsy leave. Family was a blessing and a curse. But at least she had a job she loved more than anything else.

She'd get through this just like she got through everything in her life. She was strong. She had to be. No one or nothing was going to keep her from becoming exactly who she was meant to be.

That settled, Patsy walked with confidence. She refused to allow one night of recklessness to change anything about her. Even if she couldn't get that man out of her mind—even if the thought of not being with him hurt.

She was a doctor and she'd go through many life changing decisions in her life. What she needed to do about Dr. Kyle Armistead wasn't going to be one of those decisions. That was already decided.

If only she felt better.

CHAPTER NINETEEN

"**D**R. LANDER TO OR three. Dr. Lander to OR three." The announcement flashed over her pager and cell phone at the same time. Patsy rushed down the hallway toward the operating room. She was full of energy after downing a monster-sized coffee and getting more than three hours of sleep the night before.

She stopped in the scrub room, her heart thumped at the sight of Kyle at the sinks. He looked as good as an oasis after being lost in the desert for three days. He turned and looked at her, a distant gaze in his eyes. That stopped her wandering mind. She was instantly concerned.

"Thanks for coming so fast," he told her, his voice tight.

"What's wrong?" she asked as she moved beside him, now in full work mode, not worried about the awkwardness that had been between them for well over a week.

"We have a six-month-old baby who was in a car wreck. It caught fire. His other doctors stabilized him, but the left side of his face is burned. We need to save as much of the skin as possible and seal up the wounds."

Patsy felt her blood run cold. She couldn't help but think about her own nephew and how her sister would feel if it was him on an operating table. She was shocked by how upset Kyle appeared to be by the situation, though. She didn't take him as the type of doctor to look at his patients as people rather than canvases.

"Doesn't Dr. Forbes normally handle emergencies?" she asked.

The need to scrub so thoroughly was sometimes frustrating when a patient was waiting, but adding infections to the baby's injuries wouldn't do him any good at all.

"Kian's not here, and I've worked with more children," he told her, not seeming at all offended by her question. "I want to do this case."

"I'm sorry. That was a stupid question. Thanks for including me," she told him.

"I'm your teacher," he said. "And there are no stupid questions when you're a resident. You don't learn if you don't ask." Then he walked into the OR, leaving Patsy to finish on her own. She felt slightly chastised and definitely put in her place. She needed to have respect for him as a doctor if not as a man.

She joined him a few minutes later and spent the next couple hours getting to know more about the man than she'd already known—in a positive way. He was focused and patient and a good teacher. He was also saving this child from horrific scarring that could follow him the rest of his life.

When they finished, they carefully scrubbed away the mess from the surgery before Kyle turned to her. With the surgery over, Patsy had the need to run away quickly, go back to the silence that had followed them since they'd slept together.

"Would you like to speak to the parents with me?" he asked.

"Yes," she said, without hesitation. She wasn't often asked to do this. That far outweighed her need to flee.

She followed him through the hall to a patient room where a woman lay in the bed, bandages on her head and hand, her eyes puffy and swollen, tears still falling down her cheeks. She looked as if she'd been in an accident.

A man sat next to her bed, his own eyes red and swollen. He stood as soon as they entered the room. "How's our son?" he asked, terror and hope in his voice.

Patsy stood back as Kyle approached the terrified parents. "Andrew is going to be fine," he assured them both, moving close to the mom and taking the seat next to her as he reached for her uninjured hand. "We were able to save some of the skin and get all of the burned flesh removed. After he's had some time to heal, we'll do a skin graft that I believe will attach beautifully. Not only are his vitals stable, but you'll be able to recognize your beautiful baby boy with no problem," he assured them.

The mother burst into more tears as she squeezed Kyle's hand. The father sat next to him and thanked him repeatedly.

"It's okay to let it out. You've been through a lot today. But you and your son are both going to be okay," Kyle told the mother again.

"I should've been paying more attention to traffic, and I would've seen that car. I did this," she said, her sobs making her words barely recognizable.

Kyle squeezed her fingers. "The officer said a drunk driver hit you. There was nothing you could've done to stop this," he told her. "Don't blame yourself. Work on healing so when Andrew's ready to go home you can take care of him. You've been protecting him from the beginning of his life. It might be a little rough for a few months, but you're doing a beautiful job. He's healthy and happy, and that's why it was easy for me to do his surgery. If he'd been malnourished or you hadn't been taking such good care of him, this could've gone an entirely different way."

"Thank you for that," the mother said, her sobs breaking Patsy's heart.

"Of course. It was my pleasure, and I'll be following up with him every couple of hours, and when I'm gone, the staff knows they can page me at any time. I won't let anything happen to him—not on my watch," he assured them before turning. "This is Dr. Lander. She assisted in the surgery and did a beautiful job with Andrew's stitches."

Patsy stepped forward. "Your son was in very good hands with Dr. Armistead. I've never seen a better job done or so much care put into a surgery," Patsy assured the parents.

"Thank you, Dr. Lander. Thank you so much," the father said.

Kyle continued speaking with the parents while Patsy slipped from the room, a tear sliding down her face. She wanted to think of Kyle as nothing more than a playboy plastic's doctor, but it was getting more and more difficult to look at him that way.

The care he'd shown with that baby had been beautiful, and the way he'd spoken to the parents wasn't common in a lot of doctors. But just because he was an excellent surgeon didn't mean he was a good partner.

Yes, she'd been avoiding him . . . but he hadn't done anything to stop her from doing so. As grateful as she was to do these surgeries, she'd rather not share an OR with him. It was too confusing for her already befuddled brain.

She went home that night more confused than ever, wondering what it all meant.

CHAPTER TWENTY

ONE THING ABOUT working in a hospital when you were trying to avoid the messiness of your life was that you were so busy you didn't have time to dwell on anything but work.

For the next few days Patsy did little more than pass Kyle in the hallways as she moved from patient to patient and doctor to doctor. The heated gazes exchanged between the two of them let Patsy know he was remembering their night together just as vividly as she was.

But when they were at work, sex was pushed to the back of her brain. As long as she didn't see him, she was fine.

The rare moments she was home, though . . . well, those moments were filled with images of their bodies entwined, of how it felt to be in bed with Kyle, held by him, filled with him.

Luckily she wasn't home a heck of a lot, and when she was, her time was filled with her clumsy, beautiful dog, or she was passed out, too tired to think straight, let alone agonize over something that wasn't meant to be.

Patsy learned more and more every day, and for that she was grateful. She knew her love would be emergency medicine. She enjoyed working with Doctor Kian Forbes more than any of the other surgeons. He was patient and knowledgeable, and every time a plastic surgeon was needed in the ER, he paged her.

It made her feel special.

And it had the added benefit of keeping her away from Kyle most of the time; his specialty was cosmetics, which was not what she wanted to do. Breast implants and eyelifts were great and all, but she wanted slashes and wounds and putting people back together like a puzzle. That, to her, was the most satisfying.

"You look like you're a million miles away."

Patsy's hand stilled as she worked on delicate facial stitching. She paused as she looked at Dr. Forbes, who was grinning at her.

"I might've noticed some mumbling going on there," he said with a laugh.

"I tend to talk to myself when I allow my mind to go too many places," she answered with an embarrassed shrug.

"I think we all do that," Kian told her.

"I'm sorry. I'll try not to get distracted." The patient should always come first. She didn't want Kian kicking her out of the OR because she was being foolish.

"If this is you distracted, I can't wait to see what happens when you aren't," he told her. "You're an excellent surgeon with an eye for detail."

His praise warmed her. Of course she loved working with him. He made her feel good about herself.

"Thank you for teaching me so much," Patsy said as she put the final stich in her patient then examined the area to be sure.

"It's easy to teach someone so willing to learn," Kian told her. "This is great. We're all done."

She beamed at him. He didn't have to go over anything she'd done, the greatest compliment he could give her. They'd definitely have to keep an eye on the patient and make sure everything was healing nicely, that the skin would come together without any abscesses, but for now they were finished.

She stepped away from the table and removed her gloves as they walked into the scrub room together.

"You have a few days off, don't you?" Kian asked as they stood side by side at the sink.

Patsy sighed. Too much time off wasn't good for her peace of mind. "Yeah, but I told them they could call anytime. If there are any emergencies I hope you'll page me."

Kian laughed. "You've had plenty of time here. Get refreshed. You'll be a better surgeon for it," he said.

With that Kian left and Patsy headed to the locker room. She always peeked through the door, making sure Kyle wasn't in there before she stepped inside. It was silly and foolish. It wasn't as if he was going to press her against the wall and take her right then and there . . . but the thought of him doing that made her heart thump and her blood heat.

She could try to avoid him all she wanted, but she missed him. She missed him more than she dared admit to herself.

She rushed through a shower and changed, her body so worn out she might sleep for the next twenty-four hours. That would be pure heaven. Her dog wouldn't like it too much, but he'd understand.

She needed to sleep, then she had a dinner with her sis the next day that would most likely lead to more interrogations from not only her sis, but the entire family. She'd do well to rest up before that happened.

Freedom from the walls she was grateful to be in was a light shining through the dark as Pasty quickly made her way through the hospital. She didn't know what Kyle's schedule was, but with her away from her apartment and the hospital for a few days, she'd surely pull herself together enough that when she did see him again she'd be completely fine with the situation.

Maybe they'd even end up friends.

She stepped outside, intent on hailing a cab and getting home as quickly as possible. But as she raised a hand she heard the voice that haunted her day and night only inches behind her.

"Hello, Dr. Lander. It's been a while," he said, his voice low, sexy, and intimate. She closed her eyes for the briefest of seconds, and her mind quickly took her back to his dark bedroom, making a shudder rush through her.

Trying to be as strong as she possibly could, she slowly turned, prepared for the hit to her gut from looking into his eyes. There wasn't enough time to prepare for that slow burn brewing in his gaze. Heat. Hunger. Humor. It was all there. He scanned her face, and it felt as if he'd touched her.

"Hi," she said lamely, her voice breathy as if she'd run a damn marathon.

"Have we been playing hide and seek?" he asked. She was confused. At least that made her desire temper a bit.

"What?" she asked. It felt as if it was just the two of them.

"I don't recall having a woman try so hard to avoid me," he told her. There was definite humor in his eyes, but something else lay just beneath. She'd think it was hurt, but that would be insane.

Kyle Armistead had a thousand people in his life. All he had to do was crook his finger and women would line up to be with him. There was no way Patsy's avoidance could upset him in the least little bit.

"I haven't been avoiding you," she said, forcing out a laugh. "I've been super busy." She was going to add more, but the humor in his eyes stopped her. He was very aware of her lie. "Okay, maybe I have avoided you. I haven't done this before, and I . . ."

She stopped talking and waited for him to help her out. It seemed he was willing to let her go on and on. That wasn't very gentlemanly of him.

"Haven't done what before?" he asked.

Her face instantly flamed, which ticked her off. She was a surgeon, dammit, not some naïve teenage girl after an awkward experience in the back of his daddy's truck.

"I don't sleep with co-workers or my bosses," she said, trying to sound as if it was no big deal for her to be saying this to him. "What we did was a one-time thing and well, it's awkward right now, as much as I don't want it to be." She didn't add that she couldn't look at him without thinking of his spectacular body . . . naked and hard.

She really wanted an earthquake to hit right about now, or anyone from the hospital to join them. Anything to end this torturous conversation.

"I thought we were friends," he said.

She looked at him again. "We've never been friends," she pointed out.

He smiled, but there seemed to be stress in the expression. It went away so quickly she thought she had to be imagining that. Kyle was a world-renowned plastic surgeon who had the Midas touch in the operating room. He didn't need her in his life.

"I want to be friends," he told her. "Let's have dinner and start over."

She gaped at him for a few seconds. Then she sighed. "I don't think that's a good idea. We really don't have anything in common."

"We're both surgeons," he said with a chuckle. "That's definitely something in common." Heat returned to his gaze and she knew exactly what else he was thinking about.

"There are lots of surgeons here for you to be friends with," she said.

Again that hint of hurt flashed in his eyes; it had to be her imagination, what she wanted to see. Though for the life of her she couldn't imagine why.

"But I haven't slept with any of them and then had them sneak out of my bed and avoid me afterward," he told her.

Her cheeks flamed bright red as she looked around to make sure no one had heard him. She turned back and glared.

"This isn't an appropriate talk to have here," she said. "I don't need rumors spread about me."

"I agree. We'll do dinner and talk inappropriately away from the hospital."

She was flabbergasted, but she let him take her arm and lead her toward the parking garage. They were nearly halfway to his car before she began to protest.

She stopped herself. Maybe this was a talk they needed to have. Otherwise he'd keep on making inappropriate comments at the hospital, and she knew for sure it didn't take much for the grapevine to hear in the halls. She'd never been part of the gossip discussion, but she'd heard about co-workers and didn't want the same for herself.

"I guess we're doing to dinner," she said when they reached his car. He laughed, and it made her grind her teeth. "You aren't a man who often takes no for an answer, are you?"

"No, I'm not," he said, the humor fading as he gazed intimately at her. "Especially when it's something I want."

A shudder passed through her. He couldn't mean he wanted her. That was ridiculous. Yeah, the sex had been great, and yeah he was chasing her now, but that was only because she'd been elusive. As soon as he won his prize he'd lose interest.

And that was for the best.

She didn't reply as she slipped into his car. They would have dinner, she would put her foot down, then this would all stop.

Easy.

Patsy refused to think nothing in life was quite that cut and dry. What she wanted to think about was much better.

Dinner.

That was all. Nothing more. She could do it. Then Kyle would be nothing but a distant memory.

Yeah, and she'd put down her scalpel and try space travel. That was just as likely.

Let the dinner begin.

CHAPTER TWENTY-ONE

PATSY NEVER ENJOYED dating. That might seem odd to some people, but dating wasn't relaxing, it was a lot of work. It required sharing personal information about yourself, and trying to dig out information on the other person. That wasn't something she liked or was good at.

What was the worst kind of date? Hands down, the answer was dinner. Why was the standard date a dinner at a restaurant? Why did you need to sit across the table from essentially a stranger and have everything about you judged? What kind of food would you choose? Was it kosher? We're you drinking too little or too much? Should it be white wine or red? What if you wanted a beer? What if you wanted water? Were you trying to look after your weight? The questions went on and on and on and on.

With all of that weighing on your mind, how could you relax enough at a meal to get to know another person? It made no sense to Patsy. So of course, given she was already nervous around Kyle, he goes and insists on dinner at a place with other people just dying to listen in on an awkward conversation and laugh about it later.

It actually helped calm her. It would be easy to terminate this relationship, or lack of one, if he was just another typical guy.

She'd been on dinner dates before and there hadn't been a single good memory from having dinner together.

Kyle led her into an upscale restaurant, another strike in the negative column. It was worse to go to some high-end place where she couldn't understand the menu. It didn't matter that once her sister had married into the Titan family, she'd been surrounded by wealth.

Though the Titan's were incredibly wealthy, they weren't snobby at all. Yes, she'd dined at some nice places, but her favorite memories of being with that family were pizza and game nights, theme parks, and family barbecues. Nothing spectacular happened at a fancy restaurant. Not ever.

"You seem uncomfortable. Do you not like this place?" Kyle asked as they were sat at a table.

She shrugged, trying to pull herself from negative thoughts. Patsy didn't focus on the bad. Maybe that was another strike against this man. She didn't like how it made her think about herself.

"I've never been here," she told him as she gazed at the menu; nothing on it looked appealing.

He stared at her a few moments and smiled. The waiter appeared and asked if they'd like something to drink. Patsy internally sighed. This meal would take at least two hours. She'd much rather be in her pajamas eating pizza than sit through two dull hours.

Kyle's laugh startled her out of her thoughts once more. Then he surprised her when he stood. The waiter's expression didn't change. He was obviously used to eccentric customers.

"We're leaving. Thank you," Kyle told the man.

"Is there something I can change?" the man asked, keeping his expression neutral.

"Nope. The lady obviously doesn't want to be here," Kyle told the waiter. Kyle pulled out a crisp hundred-dollar bill and handed it to the man before holding out his hand to Patsy who looked at him in confusion.

"There's no need to make a scene," she said, unsure of what to do now.

"No scene. We're going," Kyle told her.

Patsy didn't want to be there, but she was surprised Kyle had noticed. She believed she'd kept her thoughts to herself. She gave him her hand and instantly felt better as they exited the place.

"I feel bad," she whispered as they passed the hostess station.

"They aren't going out of business because we're leaving," Kyle told her. He handed his ticket to the valet and waited for his car.

"Where are we going?" she asked.

"I know a great pizza place," he said.

She wanted to kiss him, she was so relieved. And even though she still thought about those pajamas, at least pizza wouldn't take nearly as long as a five-star restaurant that turned a meal into artwork.

"How about we order it to go and have it on my balcony? We can enjoy a fire and a glass of wine with our meal and talk uninterrupted," he suggested.

Patsy was a little terrified at being at his place again, but it was as if he was reading her mind with his suggestion. Just because she went back to his place didn't mean anything would happen. She was stronger than that. She'd have pizza and maybe a couple glasses of wine, and she'd tell him in no uncertain terms this thing between them couldn't be more than casual acquaintances.

That should be easy peasy.

"I think that sounds great," she said.

He took her to a small mom and pop pizza joint, and they shared a glass of wine while they waited for their pizza. Kyle kept the conversation casual as he talked about his latest patient who'd lost nearly two hundred pounds and was having excess skin removed. Patsy hadn't done one of those surgeries, but she wanted to.

She'd met patients after their surgeries and the joy in their expressions told her how important the work was. The body was an amazing thing and truly could heal and bounce back from a lot of damage, but when the skin was stretched too far there was only so much a person could do on their own.

When Patsy had free time, she enjoyed looking at before and after pics of patients. It was satisfying to know she was a part of people's journeys in their lives. The longer she did this job the less judgmental she felt about any of it.

"What made you decide to go into this field?" she asked.

"I think it's because I've always looked at a person as more of a canvas than an actual human," he said with a chuckle. "It sounds kind of bad when I say it out loud like that."

"I don't think so," Patsy told him. "I don't look at people the same way as you, but the world needs all sorts of people in it, and at the end of the day it's no one's business what we decide to do with our own bodies. If someone wants to change something about themselves and you're willing to help them, shame on all of us for having an opinion about that."

Kyle smiled. "I've noticed a lot of change in you since you started this program," he told her.

"I've decided the world doesn't revolve around me," she said with a laugh. "And I'm trying to be a better person. I'm trying to live my life the best I can and hope others think the same way. It doesn't matter what I think of another person, it only matters how they feel about themselves."

"I agree. Sometimes I forget that basic lesson, and then I meet someone like you who reminds me," Kyle told her.

"I've seen nothing but kindness from you when it comes to your patients," she said.

"I love my patients," he said quickly. "But I'm human, and I forget those basic lessons in life. I too want to look at people without any judgment. It's not easy when we live in a world that is so quick to condemn another for things that have nothing to do with our own life."

"Why do you think that is?" Patsy asked.

"Why what is?"

"Why are we so harsh toward others?"

He sat back and thought about her question. She appreciated that, appreciated that he wasn't blowing off her words with a thoughtless reply.

"I honestly don't know. I wish I could come up with an answer," he told her. "I think it's definitely something that's taught to us somehow because we don't come out of the womb hating ourselves or anyone else. So if being negative toward others is something taught, we should be able to shift that thinking, don't you think?"

Now it was her turn to look deep inside. "I think that's easier said than done. To change a lifelong habit isn't easy."

"Nothing worthy of change is ever easy," he pointed out.

"And nothing easy is ever worth it," she said.

They smiled at each other, and for the first time Patsy felt completely comfortable with a man, completely in sync with him. And for a moment she wasn't frightened by that thought.

Their pizza was ready and they left, heading back to their apartment building. It didn't take them long to arrive.

"I'm going to change," she told him as they stepped inside, him holding the box that had tempted her the entire car ride. The smell was amazing.

"I'll wait," he told her.

"You don't need to," she said as they climbed the stairs.

"You might change your mind, and I'll end up eating this entire pizza myself."

He stood by her door, making Patsy laugh. "I don't think there's any chance of that. The smell is killing me." She reached for the box, and he held it out of her reach. She frowned at him.

"Hurry and change so we can dive in."

Rolling her eyes, she left him as she raced to her bedroom. She was in no way trying to impress this man, she assured herself. She refused to look in the mirror and tidy up her face or hair. This was just two co-workers sharing a pizza and getting an understanding of each other.

She put on sweats and her favorite raggedy college T-shirt then met him by the foyer. He looked at her as if she was wearing a skintight black dress and he was ready to strip her. That thought made her skin tingle.

"Let's go," she said, unable to look into his eyes for too long. She feared she might ignite if she did.

They were silent as they climbed to the top floor. His place was a little more organized than the last time she'd been there, no boxes in the living room anymore. A few pictures now hung on the walls. She didn't know when he'd had the time to do any of it.

She followed him to the patio doors she'd missed the last time she'd been there, and she was filled with jealousy as she stepped out on a large open balcony with a great view of the city and a large gas fire pit.

"I don't even have a small balcony," she said with a pout.

"You can use mine anytime you like," he told her.

"Tempting," she said. "There's nothing I like more than sitting outside watching the sun go down."

"Want a key?" he offered.

"Of course not," she said. This wasn't the way she'd wanted this conversation to go. Not at all.

"It's yours anytime you change your mind," he told her. She wasn't sure if he was serious or not, but she didn't want to push the issue.

They sat by the fire and finished a bottle of wine as they polished off the pizza. Sometimes she skipped an entire day of meals, grabbing snacks when she could. When she actually did slow down, she was always starving.

They continued chatting about work and life and learning a little more about each other. It grew later and as it came time to leave Patsy knew she was in trouble.

They didn't talk about the fact that their night together was a one-time thing. And as she looked at him she realized that wasn't at all what she wanted. She hated dating, she reminded herself. But this non-date had been about the most perfect night she'd experienced in a very long time.

She didn't want it to end.

From the look in his eyes, he felt the exact same way.

She had a decision to make, and she knew she had to make it quick.

CHAPTER TWENTY-TWO

PATSY FLASHED AWAKE, this time knowing exactly where she was and who she was with. Her head was clear, and she felt tingles travel through her body at what she and Kyle had done the night before.

She'd had every intention of leaving his apartment with her head held high and her clothes firmly in place. But the second she'd stood he had too, and the instant their mouths had touched, it was all over.

The protests in her head had been drowned out by the raw need filtering through her. She wanted this man, wanted what he could do to her and with her. She hadn't argued, not even once.

And they'd fallen back into his big, beautiful bed, and made love for at least two hours straight, and then once more she'd fallen asleep in the comfort of his arms.

As she lay trapped beneath the weight of his arm and leg, she tried telling herself she was glad it happened, but it certainly couldn't happen again. However, feeling his hard body next to hers, she knew she wanted it over and over again.

"Stupid. This is stupid," she muttered quietly.

He stirred and Patsy froze. If he so much as rubbed a finger across her skin she was going to explode. Kyle had awoken something in her she couldn't seem to turn off, no matter how much she tried telling herself she needed to.

When he didn't move again after a full five minutes that felt like an hour with her body on fire and her heart racing, Patsy slowly pushed his arm off her and began climbing out from beneath him.

She knew he was going to be furious with her for sneaking off again, but she was left with little choice when she kept falling into his bed. This way that awkward morning after never needed to happen. It wasn't wise to have pizza and wine with him on a romantic balcony, especially when she was very short on sleep.

She got completely untangled and was about to rise from the bed when his hand shot out and grabbed her, pulling her down on her back with him on top of her in record time.

His eyes were alert, making her realize he'd been awake the entire time she'd been attempting her escape.

"Going somewhere?" he asked, humor in his voice.

"Bathroom," she said, her voice husky as his hardness pressed between her very sensitive thighs.

"Why are you so slow and cautious if you're just using the bathroom?" he asked with a chuckle that told her he knew she was lying through her teeth.

"I didn't want to wake you," she said. "I was being considerate."

He began to gently rotate his hips, and she quickly forgot anything other than the way he made her feel.

"That's very considerate of you," he told her as he leaned down and kissed the side of her neck, his tongue hot on her skin.

"I thought so," she huskily replied.

Her legs spread beneath him without any thought on her part, and he sank fully against her, the tip of his arousal dipping inside her heat. She shook beneath him. All thoughts of fleeing vanished.

"Are you on protection?" he asked, his teasing voice gone as arousal overtook them both.

"Yes," she replied. She was a surgical resident, and there was no way she was going to have a pregnancy scare. Condoms broke. Not that she had sex often, but life happened.

"I'm clean," he told her. "Do you trust me?" The fact that he was asking softened her more than anything else they'd done together. He took her at her word. That meant a lot.

"Yes," she said, realizing she did trust him.

He smiled before dropping his head and taking her mouth in a heated kiss and at the same time he sank fully within her hot folds. She sighed into his mouth as she reached up and took his head in her hands, needing to be as close to him as possible.

Moments ago she'd been trying to run from this man, and now she couldn't get close enough to satisfy the raging hunger burning throughout her body. He gave her something she'd never had before. She feared what would happen to her when it was taken away.

For now it didn't matter because she was right where she wanted to be and with exactly who she wanted to be with. He made slow and steady love to her, and then he carried her into the bathroom for a nice hot shower that she hoped he'd join her in.

She was falling fast, and it might not be a good thing, but it didn't matter. Because no matter how much she tried to fight it, she kept falling into his arms. Maybe it was exactly where she was meant to be.

And maybe it was time to turn off her brain.

CHAPTER TWENTY-THREE

THERE WAS NO better place for Kyle than right where he was. His world had seemed to be constantly spinning out of control until he felt the touch of this one woman. He'd given up a prestigious career, moved back home, and had still felt restless, as if he was missing something.

And then Patsy Lander stepped into his life.

He was done fighting it, done questioning it. He had to make her his. He didn't think he could let her go. Once certainly wasn't enough, and twice had only whetted his appetite.

The shower heated quickly, and he stood back as the hot water slid over Patsy's lush body. She was sheer perfection, and he couldn't get enough of her. She gazed at him as he watched her internal battle.

She was fighting her feelings for him, but he wasn't worried about the outcome. What they had was special. He knew that beyond a shadow of a doubt. They could fight it as much as they wanted, but at the end of the day they'd be together because they couldn't manage to stay apart.

He couldn't stand not to touch her for a second longer so he moved close, pulling her into his arms. The feel of her there reminded him how very much alive he was. She tried not looking at him, but it was magical when her head lifted, and her eyes connected with his. There was a struggle in her deep beautiful dark depths, but she was submitting to him, submitting to them.

He lowered his head, kissing her softly, easily, as if he had all the time in the world. He wanted to erase her doubts and fears. He took his time, and it didn't take long for her to reach up and cup his face, pulling him tighter as she fiercely kissed him back.

"I need you," he told her. He would hand over his power, give her anything she wanted. A shudder passed through her and he knew there was no fight left in her.

"Then take me," she said, her body melting against his. He'd had her fifteen minutes earlier but his body responded to her request as if he hadn't had sex in years. He was hard and throbbing and ready to push her against the wall and take her over and over again.

Kyle stepped back and grabbed the soap, running his fingers over every beautiful surface of her silky skin. She returned the favor, her touch unsure at first then growing more confident as her fingers circled his throbbing erection and pumped it a few times.

"Enough," he growled in a low voice as he let the water run over them long enough to rinse the suds away. Then he lifted her, kissing her hard before walking from the shower, their bodies wet, leaving a trail of water from the bathroom to the bedroom.

He took her to the fireplace and set her down in front of it, grabbed a blanket and laid it on the floor before looking at her with hunger ravishing his entire body. Her body, wet and ready, was the most beautiful thing he'd ever seen.

"Lie down," he told her. Her immediate compliance made him harden even more. He clenched his fingers in an effort to calm his raging hormones.

She gazed at the fire and the glow from the embers made him want to grab his camera. Everything about this moment was perfect.

"Look at me," he told her, and she slowly turned her head, her eyes heated, her skin damp and pink. "Spread your legs." She did so immediately. He stepped closer.

As much as he liked looking at her, tasting her was even better. Their eyes never breaking the connection, he dropped to his knees in front of her spread legs. He ran his fingers over her thighs, enjoying the tremble in them.

Only then did he look away from her beautiful face so he could trace his gaze over the rest of her. He bent over and ran his tongue along the smooth skin of her inner thigh, loving how open she was to him. She squirmed beneath him and moaned.

He wanted to bring her so much pleasure she'd never think of any other man but him. He wanted to own her, body, soul, and spirit. He wanted to consume her just as she was consuming him. He was falling for her so deeply he should run in the other direction.

But his feelings for her ensured he'd never do that.

Reaching down, he ran a finger along her sweet pink folds and her hips arched off the floor as she silently begged for more than a light touch. He wanted to tease her, draw it out, but he didn't know how long he could. Slipping his finger inside her, she clenched around him, and all he could think about was how good it felt when her body grabbed his thickness like that.

He added another finger and began pumping in and out of her body as he lowered his head, needing the taste of her on his tongue. He sucked her swollen flesh as he moved his fingers in and out of her faster and faster.

Her pleasure sounded in the room as his erection pulsed in time to her moans. She exploded around his fingers, and he tasted her orgasm on his tongue. It nearly caused him to lose it right there.

He took a deep breath, but that only made him inhale her scent. He knew he had to take her, knew foreplay had to end. Still, he drew out her orgasm, waiting for every ounce of pleasure to be wrung from her before he slowly made his way up her body, tasting her hips, her stomach, and the undersides of her full breasts.

She was quivering again, her fire stoked once more by the time he was lying against her, their mouths mere centimeters apart. She was panting beneath him, her eyes wild, her mouth parted.

"Tell me exactly what you want," he demanded as the tip of his arousal rested against her hot, wet folds.

"I need you inside me," she said, her voice barely recognizable. It was the sweetest sound ever.

He leaned down and kissed her hard, the time for talking, for games, far over. She kissed him back, their tongues tangling, their mouths fitting together perfectly. Slowly, he dipped into her hot folds a couple of inches then pulled out. The feeling was both excruciating and pleasurable.

"Please," she begged. That one word set him off, and Kyle thrust fully into her, making both of them gasp. It was sweet heaven being buried fully inside her heat.

He didn't rest long but pulled out and plunged forward again, over and over, building pleasure for both of them. And then she ripped her lips from his as a scream wrenched out of her, and her tight heat clenched around him.

Her hips arched higher as she shook over and over again, her nipples peaked against his chest, her skin flushed and hot, her face contorted in pure ecstasy. She was so beautiful he couldn't imagine ever being with another person again.

With that thought, Kyle let go, pumping his release inside her, then holding on as if he'd never let go. Neither of them moved as they tried to grasp the meaning of all of this. They both knew there was more going on than sex. It was a connection that wasn't easily found.

"I want to be with you this weekend," he told her.

She was silent for long enough he worried he was misreading her, seeing what he wanted to see instead of what was truly there.

"I have to go to my sister's tomorrow," she told him quietly.

"Then I'll come with you. We have the day off." He waited. He wanted to insist, but he also wanted her to want him there.

"Okay," she said. The fight had left her. Maybe sex truly was the key to happiness. He'd keep her in bed when they weren't sleeping or working, and they'd be fine. Hell, he could sneak her off to a bed at work once in a while too. There were plenty of them around.

"We need more sleep," he told her, his body satisfied enough to allow him to rest.

"Mmm," she murmured, already passing out beneath him.

Kyle chuckled before standing, enjoying the protest on her lips. He easily lifted her and carried her to his bed.

"Don't try to escape again," he told her.

She immediately curled up against him and was asleep in seconds. He was right behind her. They were exactly where they needed to be.

CHAPTER TWENTY-FOUR

PATSY WAS IN a sex coma. There was no other explanation for her submissiveness to whatever Kyle wanted. They'd had sex four times in a ten-hour period and her body still wanted more. She wasn't sure she could take more as she was sore from her head to the tips of her toes.

She flexed her toes while they drove closer to her sister's house. She didn't know toes could get sore. But sure enough, even her toes hurt. She assumed it was because she'd been clenching them so hard as one orgasm after another had overtaken her from his talented mouth, fingers, and her most favorite part of him.

Somehow he'd managed to not only get her to invite him to her sister's house, but to do it gladly. She'd gone from being determined to make their relationship nothing more than co-workers to not wanting to be away from him for a single minute.

Yep. Definitely a sex coma.

There was no other explanation.

"If you keep having thoughts like the ones your having I'm going to pull this car over, and we'll be arrested for indecent exposure," he said, his voice tight, his fingers gripping the steering wheel like it was a lifeline on a sinking boat.

"You can't possibly read my thoughts," she told him.

He laughed tightly. "You are far more transparent than you realize. The little hums coming out of your throat right now are driving me mad and the way you keep shifting, rubbing your thighs together, tells me you're hot and bothered . . . and wet and ready." He finished his words with a tight growl that had a surge of moisture dripping from the place he'd just been referring to.

Boldly she reached over and danced her fingers up his thigh and over the bulge in his pants. He turned to look at her for the briefest of moments as if she was insane, and the car swerved. She let out a little squeak and pulled her hand away.

He reached for her hand and grabbed it, setting it back on his thigh, though a safe distance from that bulge.

"You're killing me," he said. "But what a way to go."

"I don't know what's happening to me," she told him. "I've never felt like this, never enjoyed sex before." It was completely perplexing and being a doctor she didn't like the feeling.

He laughed. "I'm glad to be the one to bring out the sex vixen in you, but we've got to change the subject because we're only a few minutes away from your family's house and I don't want to get the crap kicked out of me if they find us naked in my car."

She laughed this time, feeling free and confident. He made her feel beautiful and desired, and she didn't want to think about tomorrow or the next day. For once in her life she just wanted to live in the moment.

"Are you ready for this? My family is quite intimidating," she told him. She was almost afraid to go now. At first she'd thought it might be good, she'd simply chase him away. But now she was afraid of that happening.

She was sure this would eventually fizzle out. It had to run its course. But she wasn't ready for that yet. If he ran from her before she could figure out this new side of her, she feared she'd never be willing to try another relationship again. Not that this was a relationship. This was just sex—amazing sex—but just sex.

"I'm looking forward to getting to know your sister. I know how much she means to you," he told her. That confused her as well. Why was that important to him? If it truly was just sex, why did he need to know her family? Something to think about later.

They pulled up to the house, and Patsy looked at the enormous structure. Her sis had been married to Ryan Titan for ten years and Patsy still wasn't quite used to it. They'd had nothing growing up and now luxury was a normal part of their lives. It was odd. Patsy didn't like bringing people to her sis's house because she didn't want them to know this side of her life. But because Kyle was used to the same lifestyle it was less intimidating.

He climbed from the car and came around to open her door. "One kiss," he insisted, pulling her into his arms. She didn't try to resist, needing his kiss as much as she needed oxygen.

A throat cleared, which was probably a good thing because as soon as Kyle's mouth touched hers, Patsy forgot there was a life outside of the two of them. Slowly, she broke away from him, loving the enraptured look on his face. She turned to find her sister grinning like a dang loon at the two of them.

"You're late," Nicole said with a laugh. "But I can see why." Her gaze swept over Kyle, who placed his arm around Patsy in a possessive manner. She was sure her sister noticed.

"I didn't tell you a specific time so I can't be late," Patsy said. It took effort but she pulled away from Kyle to give her sister a hug.

"I planned on you being here at noon so I count it as late," Nicole said. She turned back to Kyle. "Thank you for joining us. We always love more company." Patsy watched a bit of shock on his face when Nicole gave him a hug. Nicole had always been a touchy feely person and Patsy was used to it.

If he was going to run, it was a foregone conclusion, one that she couldn't change, so Patsy wouldn't sit there and analyze everything that happened over the next few hours.

"Are the rest of the gang members standing on the other side of the door?" Patsy asked. Nicole turned back to her with a chuckle.

"You know they are. I threatened all of them if they dared step foot outside until I had you to myself for a minute or two."

Patsy turned to Kyle. "Ryan would literally walk over hot coals for my sister, so we could be out here for an hour and he wouldn't step through that door if she told him not to." There weren't many loves as great as that shared between her sister and brother-in-law.

"Sounds like a smart man," Kyle said as he winked at Nicole, who giggled.

"Yes, and kind and loving and wonderful," Nic said. She turned back to Patsy. "I'm not seeing you enough lately, and I don't like it. I'm glad you're home. I love that you have a great job, but family time needs to be a priority."

"I know. I'm sorry. I'll try to do better," Patsy said. She hated hurting her sister. And she truly did miss her when she was away too long.

A loud whine came from the car, and Patsy laughed as she rushed back and opened the door.

"I'm sorry, boy." Eeyore jumped down with an accusatory stare. She never forgot her dog, dang it.

"My fault. I distracted you," Kyle told her. The dog gave him a pouty look that had both of them laughing.

Eeyore quickly recovered from the mishap and sauntered over to Nicole, waiting for his pat on the head. Then he sniffed her pocket, and she laughed as she pulled out a bone and handed it to him.

"Nic always has treats for Eeyore. She takes care of him when I have to travel," Patsy told Kyle.

"Ah, he's not spoiled or anything," Kyle told her with a laugh.

"Not at all," she said.

"We'd better get inside before the boys have a heart attack. I hope you're up for a CIA style interrogation," Nicole said as she winked at Kyle.

"Bring it on," Kyle told her.

"Oh, I like you already," Nic said as she placed one arm through Patsy's and one through Kyle's. "This day will be so much fun."

The pure glee in Nic's voice scared Patsy. What plans did her family have for Kyle? She suddenly was a bit afraid. This could go badly, very, very badly. But there was no going back now. They were there and it was do-or-die time.

CHAPTER TWENTY-FIVE

THE BOYS MUST'VE scrambled when they knew the three of them were coming into the house because they weren't at the front door. Pasty grinned at Nic, who winked at her and then Kyle.

"They're going to pretend they've been in the den the entire time. We can let them get away with that. You're going to be a hot topic around here for a while. Patsy doesn't ever bring men home, not since the boys kept chasing them away when she was a teen."

"Nicole," Pasty grumbled, "can you try a little bit not to embarrass me? Kyle and I are friends and work together."

"Yeah, just friends huh?" Nic asked with another laugh. "I don't normally give friends hot, wet kisses."

"Well, um, some friends kiss," Patsy said, her voice getting lower as Kyle laughed then reached down and smacked her butt. She looked at him in horror.

"My brother-in-law will murder you if you do that in front of him," she warned.

"I'm not afraid," Kyle said, confidence shining in his eyes.

"You should be," Patsy said with a bit of glee. She truly didn't want him chased away, but she wouldn't mind that cockiness knocked down a peg or two.

They stepped into the den where they found three men chatting as they held beers. They turned as if surprised they had visitors. Patsy laughed aloud.

"You aren't fooling anyone," she said as she let go of her sister and rushed over to Ryan. He wasn't just her sis's husband, he was her big brother. She truly loved him to the moon and back.

"What? We've been waiting for you all day. Your sister's been going crazy," he told her as he hugged her tight then pushed her back so he could examine her. "You look like you finally got some sleep. I like it."

She grinned at him. "If you weren't always worrying about me, maybe you wouldn't have those circles under your eyes where I got rid of mine," she said.

"It's a brother's job to worry," he assured her. She hugged him again.

"Come meet my friend, Kyle Armistead," she said.

Ryan's smile fell away, and she nearly laughed at the stern look that came over his expression. She'd seen that look on his face many times before. If Kyle wasn't made of the good stuff, he'd take a look at Ryan and run screaming. Patsy had lost many a suitor because of Ryan, and she just figured they weren't good enough if they were that easily intimidated.

But Kyle walked straight up to Ryan and held out his hand. "Thanks for the invite. I hear it's your birthday," he said.

Ryan didn't say a word for a moment, and Patsy found herself holding her breath, but then a chuckle from Derek and Drew, who were sitting on the couch, came through, and the tension seemed to break.

"I always like to meet Patsy's friends. She means the world to this family," Ryan told Kyle. It was a clear message she wasn't alone.

Patsy enjoyed that message, but she wanted to interfere, to tell her family not to chase this one away. She had to remind herself if he was the type of guy to be chased away, she wouldn't want to be with him.

And she also had to admit she was really falling for him. It was a mistake on a colossal level. She knew that. But like a runaway train, there was no stopping it, so she might as well embrace the moment.

"Family's important," Kyle said without missing a beat. "Now, that we've ensured I know Patsy's well looked after, are you going to offer me a beer?"

Derek and Drew outright laughed this time as they stood and moved over to where Kyle and Ryan were sizing each other up. Finally Ryan smiled.

"Okay, let's have a beer and get the grill going. We're going to have a few dozen people here soon since my wife likes a party."

"Sounds good," he said. Then he moved over to Patsy and gave her a quick, possessive kiss. Nothing inappropriate. "Wish me luck. I'm getting interrogated," he said in a mock whisper the entire room heard.

"Good luck," she told him. She realized she was holding her breath as he was pulled away from her.

"I like him a lot," Nic said with a gleam in her eyes. "Now it's time for *your* interrogation." She dragged Patsy to the kitchen where Jasmine and Trinity were waiting.

"Can't we just skip this part?" Patsy begged, knowing it wouldn't do any good whatsoever.

"Not a chance. We want all the details. That man is smoking hot," Trinity said. "And I think he might be the first one to stand up to the boys."

"Oh, calling out Ryan and demanding a beer was my happy moment of the day," Trinity said with a chuckle.

"Yeah, Ryan will be grumbling about that later tonight," Nicole said. "And it's so worth it. Those boys get a little too arrogant sometimes, and they need another man thrown into the mix to remind them they're not gods every once in a while."

"Amen to that," Trinity said. "But that's what we're here for."

"True. Do you think Patsy's met her match?" Nic asked.

"I'm standing right here," Patsy told the women who ignored her.

"I think she might have this time," Jasmine said as she continued peeling eggs.

"Ooh, I'm thinking a spring wedding," Nic said.

"I'm *right* here," Patsy said again with a glare at her sister and honorary aunts.

"Yes, you are dear. Should we measure now or later for the gown?" Trinity asked with a giggle.

"You're all hopeless," Patsy said, finally joining in with the laughter. "If I tell you how great the sex is will you stop talking about weddings?"

The absolute delight on all three of their faces instantly won her this argument. They stopped pretending to work and grabbed a bottle of wine as Patsy told them all about her strange relationship with one Kyle Armistead.

CHAPTER TWENTY-SIX

TWILIGHT ON THE outskirts of Seattle was beautiful. It wasn't as great as it was in the country because the city lights filtered the sky, but at Ryan and Nicole's place the stars could be seen. She rarely saw stars in downtown Seattle.

She was well fed and had laughed more this evening than she had in a very long time. There had only been a few mishaps during the night. She hadn't been thrilled when Darcy Pently had shown up in a tight skirt with her breasts hanging halfway out of her cropped shirt. Patsy had gone to school with the evil girl, who thought it was fun to steal as many boyfriends as humanly possible before she turned thirty.

But she was the sister of one of Ryan's closest friends, and he couldn't very well tell his friend not to bring his slutty sister along. Patsy had no doubt whatsoever Ryan would do that if Patsy ever complained, but she wouldn't. No way. She loved Ryan far too much to put him in that position.

Nicole didn't do anything on a small scale, so after all the food was eaten, a local band set up and music began. People milled about the dance floor, and Patsy couldn't help but smile. This was a sight she'd seen many times through her years at the Titan house.

"How are you doing, young lady?"

Patsy's smile grew to the point her cheeks ached as she spun around. She knew that voice all too well. She didn't hesitate as she threw herself into Joseph Anderson's arms.

"I haven't seen you in forever. Why weren't you here for dinner? I would've insisted I get to sit next to you," she said with true joy.

Joseph Anderson was known to the world as a business mogul. But Patsy had known him for as long as her sis had been with Ryan, and he'd come to the hospital every day after she'd had her heart surgery. He might have a loud voice and a way of intimidating others like nobody's business, but to her he was a giant teddy bear and the only grandfather figure she had in her life. She'd love to be a member of his family, though in a way she already felt she was.

"Oh, my life's been chaotic lately," Joseph said with a smile. "I found out I have a slew of nephews who need a firm hand and some guidance," he added with a twinkle.

Patsy smiled in delight. "What? I haven't heard anything about lost relatives," she said. "If there were newly discovered Andersons, it'd be in every newspaper in the country."

"No one knows yet, so you keep quiet," Joseph said. "I'm sharing a deep secret with you. My uncle, who wasn't a good man, married a woman far too young for him," Joseph grumbled. "It's just sick in my opinion." He said a few curse words about the evil uncle, but then he smiled. "But the woman was a good mother, and she gave me new nephews, so it all worked out. I only recently found out about them, so I want them to get to know me since their father and I didn't have a good relationship."

"I can't believe with all that going on you managed to make it over here," she said.

"I always have time for you, young lady," he chastised.

"It's Ryan's birthday, not mine," she said, feeling cherished.

"Well, I found out you were finally coming home, so I had to make an appearance."

She threw her arms around him again. "I love you, Joseph. I'll come by on my next day off, and we can have lunch. I miss our talks."

"I love you too, sweet girl," he said. She saw a suspicious sparkle in his eyes, but he turned away and when he looked at her again, his eyes were bright and inquisitive. The sentimental moment was over. "Now tell me about this young man you brought home with you."

It wasn't a question, it was a demand. "We just work together, but . . ." she trailed off. She wasn't exactly sure how to finish that sentence. There was no way in hell she was telling a man she considered a grandfather about how great sex was with Kyle.

"But you're feeling things for him," Joseph prodded.

"Maybe a little, but we aren't a couple," she said.

"Well if it matters, he's a good man," Joseph told her. She narrowed her eyes as she gazed at him. He didn't so much as blink.

"Did you check him out?" she asked, her hands on her hips.

"Of course I checked him out, just like I'm supposed to," Joseph told her.

She wanted to be mad, but there was no way she could, not with that sweet smile on his lips. "You're terrible, Joseph Anderson. I should go and tell Katherine right now."

They both turned toward a delightful laugh coming from the woman they were talking about. She was the love of Joseph's life, and he didn't ever try to hide how he felt about her.

"Don't you dare. I'm out of the doghouse at the moment," he said, his eyes shining as he gazed at his wife.

"Then quit meddling and maybe you'll stay out of it," Patsy told him.

"I can't promise anything," he admitted.

Patsy laughed, unable to stay mad at this man even if he was meddling in her life. She was used to that by now. As a matter of fact, she'd be lost if these strong men she called family didn't meddle. Maybe it was their way of showing how much they loved her.

"Speaking of your young man, where did he run off to?" Joseph asked. "I was hoping to chat with him."

Patsy laughed again. "Don't you dare," she said. She looked around but didn't see Kyle. "He probably got a page and is off making a phone call. I'd better go find him. It's either that or one of my family members has him cornered and he needs rescued."

"Then rescue away, fair lady. I'm going to take Katherine for a spin on that dance floor."

Patsy hugged him one more time then set off to find Kyle. She was more than ready to get him alone. The day had been about as perfect as it could be.

She didn't know that was all about to turn on her so badly it would feel as if she'd been stabbed straight through the heart.

CHAPTER TWENTY-SEVEN

PATSY WANDERED THROUGH her sister's massive property looking for Kyle, and the longer it took the more insecure she felt about it. This was ridiculous. What were they to each other? Nothing, really.

They'd had great sex—really, *really* great sex. And he'd made her laugh and was an excellent teacher. They'd had a couple of what she guess she could consider dates. But most of their relationship had been running from each other. And they certainly weren't committed to one another. They hadn't talked about tomorrows. Still, he'd wanted to come with her to a family event. That meant something, didn't it?

Was it possible to fall in love with someone without knowing it? Was it possible to happen so quickly? She was so dang confused about how she was feeling. Part of her wanted to simply enjoy the moment. She had plans, and they didn't include a wealthy doctor who she didn't trust not to end up breaking her heart. But slowly he'd wedged himself beneath her tough exterior. And that was the problem.

Now she was anxious because she wanted to be with him and didn't know where he was. It made her incredibly uncomfortable. She decided it was best to give up.

Then she heard voices—and froze.

She knew that giggling female voice anywhere. Darcy. Her gut clenched when a sexy deep baritone responded to the woman's obvious flirtation. Peeking around a corner, she found Kyle standing far too close to be appropriate to the woman who'd made Patsy's life hell through high school.

She was about to turn away when she heard her own name. Fighting tears she felt frozen to the spot as Darcy looked her way. Patsy was pretty sure the woman hadn't seen her, but Darcy moved the extra two inches closer to Kyle as she raised a perfectly manicured nail and ran it down the center of Kyle's chest. He didn't push her away.

Why this was upsetting Patsy so much, she wasn't sure. This was exactly who Kyle was. She'd known that from the day she'd met him. He wasn't doing anything against his nature, and he wasn't committed to Patsy anyway. But it still felt like betrayal, since they had come to the party together—the party at her sister's house.

Patsy wanted to run away but Darcy said her name, and she needed to know what they were talking about. Somewhere in the back of her mind a voice was screaming at her that no good could come out of eavesdropping.

But still she stayed.

"You realize I'm here with Patsy, right?" Kyle asked. Patsy's heart thumped. Maybe this wasn't as bad as it appeared.

"It's loud out there and the band is terrible," Darcy said. "Besides I wanted to talk to you about something." The woman was a master seductress all the way from the position she was in, to the flirty gestures of her fingers, and the way she licked her perfectly painted red lips.

Who could resist that? Half the time Patsy didn't have time for makeup, let alone time to learn all those little things women did to draw attention to themselves. She'd told herself she didn't want to be that kind of woman; she didn't need to be desired. But seeing the man who'd rocked her world so intently staring at another woman made Patsy rethink that thought. She wondered what it would be like to have a man so completely enamored with her.

"What do you want to talk about?" he asked. Patsy couldn't tell if he was into the conversation or not. She could see he wasn't pulling away though.

"I heard Patsy's on a strict career path; she has no interest in relationships. Why would you want to come here with her?" Darcy asked, parts of her body in constant contact with his.

"That isn't any of your business," he told her.

She reached up and ran a hand over the back of his neck, and Patsy wondered if she was going to throw up. Kyle didn't push the woman away. His hands reached out and gripped her hip. The sight was utter betrayal.

"I've seen your work. I need a new doctor to get a few things done," Darcy told him. "And I only choose the best."

Kyle laughed and Darcy smiled at him as if the two of them were in on a joke together. With the perfection of Darcy's body, Patsy understood why he was laughing. It was obvious she didn't need plastic surgery.

"I'm booked up for a long time, and you don't need work done anyway," he told her.

She coyly smiled at him as she moved a bit closer.

"Ah, you're too sweet, doc, but there's always room for improvement. I refuse to grow old gracefully. I like who I am, and I'm not afraid to enhance what God has already given me."

Kyle laughed again. "That's how I make a living," he told her.

The friendly banter between the two of them was worse than the touching in Patsy's opinion. Darcy was the trophy wife, the type of woman Kyle would one day marry. She'd be on his arm looking absolutely perfect, the ultimate doctor's wife. That wasn't who Patsy was. She'd never be content to be a trophy. She wanted to be spectacular in her career and have her life matter. She wanted her own name to have meaning, not just be some man's wife.

"I bet you're planning on some procedures with Patsy, squeezing her into your busy schedule," she told him with a perfect pout.

Patsy froze, her insecurities rising. She knew she wasn't flawless, but she'd never considered having any work done. She'd chosen this job because she wanted to help people, not change them. She hated the scar on her chest from her heart transplant, but she hadn't thought Kyle cared. Maybe she'd been wrong. His next words broke her heart.

"What work do you think she needs done?" he asked, his voice nothing more than conversational as if he was describing any patient. He was talking about her with a woman who had always hated Patsy. It was a terrible thing to do, and Patsy wanted to reveal herself, to tell them both to go to hell, but she didn't budge.

"That nasty scar on her chest looks like it was done by a butcher. That could definitely be fixed, though I'm not sure there's much that can be done, but with the way she works all the time, I've noticed she's put on a few pounds. I'm sure things are also beginning to sag and need some lifting," she told him with her perfected laugh.

Kyle laughed at the words and Patsy's last bit of confidence in him and whatever it was they had together slipped away quicker than smoke off the end of a cigarette. She was crushed.

"Hmm, you think so, huh?" he asked, his voice almost a purr.

Darcy reached around him and Patsy was done. There was no way she was going to stand there and watch the two of them make out, possibly have sex right there on her sister's property. She had stood there long enough to know all she needed to know.

Whatever she'd had with Kyle was over. That was more than clear. She didn't want to spend a moment longer with him than she had to.

She turned and walked away, the sound of Darcy's giggle following her for too long. She fought tears as she sought out her sister, who was busy with the party. She found her laughing with a group of friends and Patsy didn't want to ruin the festivities so she turned to the house and decided to call a cab.

She wrote a quick note while waiting, telling her sister she had been paged to work and to please make her excuses. Then she grabbed her dog and slipped away before anyone found her.

She was proud that she didn't allow tears to fall until she returned to the city and made it to the safety of her bed where Eeyore snuggled with her, somehow knowing she needed the comfort.

She hadn't had an affair with Kyle. It had been two co-workers seeking pleasure. It obviously had run its course. As soon as Patsy convinced herself of that she'd feel a whole lot better.

Kyle tried calling her several times that night, but after the third try she turned off her phone and found solace in sleep. She had to gear up for the next time she saw him, because, although it wasn't fair, she *would* have to see him again.

There was no way she'd allow him the victory of knowing how badly she hurt from what he'd done. She was too strong for that. She wouldn't give him or Darcy the satisfaction of knowing they'd affected her. And soon she might be able to convince herself she was perfectly fine.

CHAPTER TWENTY-EIGHT

KYLE WAS DUMFOUNDED when he didn't find Patsy anywhere. He tried calling her and was pretty sure she was deliberately sending him to voicemail. He found himself at her family's house with no sign of her.

Sure, he'd gotten distracted visiting with people, but up until an hour before he'd been very aware of her location at all times. She'd seemed content, smiling more than he'd seen her smile before, and giving him hungry glances from across the yard.

He'd been having to be very careful with his thoughts as he was at her family's house and he didn't want to be thrown off the roof for lustful thoughts over her. He'd thought about dragging her into a dark corner somewhere, but was pretty sure he'd be murdered if they were caught with their pants down.

And then all the sudden she had just disappeared.

When he tried calling for the second time, Nicole approached him with a rueful expression.

"I hope you're having a good time," she said.

"Yes, but I can't find Patsy anywhere," he told her. "It's getting late so I thought we should head out."

"Oh." Now Nicole looked slightly embarrassed. "I thought she would've told you," she said as she looked behind her.

"Told me what?" he asked.

"She left a note that the hospital paged her. She left about thirty minutes ago."

There was a look in Nicole's eyes that told Kyle she wasn't buying that excuse any more than he was. It was something very easy to verify.

"Thank you," he told Nicole and walked away. He didn't want to be rude, but he was furious.

He called the hospital and sure enough, Patsy hadn't been called in. He was lost on why she'd left the way she had with that excuse. What had happened? Was she done with whatever it was between them? Up until an hour before everything had been perfect, or as perfect as it got for him.

He didn't do games. Hell, Kyle had never done a relationship before if he were being honest. But he really didn't do games. He tried calling her again, attempting to be patient—and failing.

The longer she ignored him, the more irritated he became. What was she up to? He deserved an explanation. The entire ride back to his apartment, his anger grew.

He parked and immediately went to her door, knocking loudly. He heard Eeyore bark, so he knew she was in there. But she didn't answer. He tried calling her again, but it went straight to voicemail.

His anger went icy cold.

He was done.

Kyle had never played games with a woman, and he wasn't going to start now just because said woman was great in bed. That was all they had together. It wasn't worth navigating a landmine of crap to see her again. She liked to run, and maybe it was so she could be chased. But she was messing with the wrong guy if that was what she wanted. He was done chasing anyone.

She'd told him from the beginning she wasn't interested in a relationship. He'd been the one with the thick skull, wanting to be with her. He'd become obsessed with her in the short time he'd known her, and it had led to nothing but trouble.

He went to his own place and snarled out loud when he stepped into his bedroom and her scent hung heavy in the air.

His desire to see her, touch her, demand an explanation from her overwhelmed him.

With a fever, he stripped his bed, throwing the sheets into the laundry room before he remade his bed. But as he lay down that night her scent still hung in the air, invading him.

He wasn't going to be able to turn off what he felt for her as easily as he'd been able to with others. He might be in more trouble with this woman than he was willing to deal with.

Dammit!

He wished life would go back to the simplicity it had been before he'd decided he was unhappy, before he'd uprooted everything. Now he wasn't sure who he was anymore.

He was putting that on Patsy Lander as much as everything else. He kept telling himself over and over how done he was. But as the night wore on, not allowing him sleep, he wondered if he could keep that promise to himself.

He deserved an explanation at least. Why was she that way? He didn't get it. She had a beautiful family, and yes, Kyle hadn't been the best at maintaining relationships in his past, but he'd been nothing but good to Patsy.

He shouldn't care.

But he did.

Best case scenario would be if he could push her from this thoughts. That would be a hell of a lot easier said than done. She'd wedged herself inside his head and . . . his heart, if he were being totally honest, and he wasn't sure she'd be easy to push out.

He'd never tried so hard with a woman, and she was constantly running from him. Most men would've moved on long ago. But then again, he'd never felt such a connection with a woman. There was an Ed Shernan song he'd found himself listening to a lot lately that talked about how people fell in love. Could it truly be as simple as the touch of a hand? He didn't know. All he knew he wanted to be done with her, wanted to stop torturing himself. But it wasn't that cut and dry.

He was going to give it one hell of a good try though. He didn't get relief until pure exhaustion pulled him under.

A new day was about to start long before he was ready.

CHAPTER TWENTY-NINE

PATSY FELT LIKE a burglar as she carefully walked the halls of the hospital she'd been so excited to work at not that long ago. She peeked around corners, listened for the sound of one particular male voice that had her stomach clenching when she heard it, and avoided the locker room as if it was a quarantine zone.

In short, she was tired, miserable, and unfocused on her job. As one day turned into two, and that turned into a week, she became grumpier and grumpier, and all of the blame went on one particular man.

She'd told him she didn't want a relationship, told him workplace affairs never worked out, told him it was a bad idea. She'd been right. The few times she'd managed to avoid him, she'd heard his voice—his very normal, non-affected voice—and her rage had grown.

He was fine. He was completely, utterly fine, while she felt as if her world was tumbling down, one stone at a time.

She could try to transfer, but that would be nearly impossible without hurting her career. Yes, she could go to Ryan and ask for help, but she wanted to do things on her own, and she wasn't letting some cheap sex alter her entire plans.

She *would* get over her feelings toward that pompous doctor. She hated allowing him to affect her as much as he had. It was foolish. He obviously didn't give a damn, so why in the world did she give him power over her?

One thing she knew for sure: she wasn't going to ever have sex with another co-worker again, let alone get in a relationship with one. No way. Not a chance.

The worst that had occurred during the miserable week was running into him twice in the hallway. He hadn't tried to turn away. Why should he? He didn't think he'd done anything wrong. In all honestly, he hadn't lied to her. He'd never told her they were exclusive. She knew who he was, but knowing that didn't change how she felt. It sucked.

Seeing him made her burn. When he looked at her, coldness in those dark eyes, she fought tears. It was foolish. Life would be much easier if she didn't care. She'd feel that way soon. She needed time.

"Earth to Patsy," Nurse Sammy said with a laugh.

Patsy snapped out of her thoughts and turned toward the young, perky nurse who had a way with kids.

"I'm sorry, Sammy. I'm not getting enough sleep," she told the woman.

"I hear ya. When I decided to go into the medical field I didn't realize that meant regular twelve hour shifts," Sammy said. "And you work more than that. I don't know how any of you do it."

"I think it's because we don't have a choice. When you love medicine there's nothing else that will satisfy you," Patsy said.

"I know. My mother can't understand how puss pockets and gashes fascinate me. I go home and talk about a really cool boil I got to drain and my family turns green and looks at me like I'm insane. I don't get it. It doesn't get better than that for me," Sammy said, a gleam in her eyes that had Patsy chuckling a bit. It felt good.

"Well, you have plenty of co-workers who are more than glad to hear about your creepiest cases," Patsy assured her.

"Yeah, but then someone here always has a better story, and I'm jealous," Sammy said with her own laugh.

"True. Maybe we can all have a competition to see who gets the creepiest case in a thirty day period," Patsy told her.

Sammy's eyes lit up. "Oh, that's brilliant! But no doctors are allowed in the contest because you will, of course, get all the best stuff. But I'm so proposing that to the rest of the nurses." It looked as if Sammy wanted to run off right then and there and start the contest. Patsy might've started a war.

"Have fun and let me know the winner," Patsy told her.

"I will for sure. Now, before I forget, you've been traded to Dr. Armistead's service tonight and tomorrow. Dr. Kelly complained he wasn't getting any ER time; you were hogging it all."

Patsy's skin went cold. She was supposed to work in the ER the rest of the week with Dr. Forbes. That was her safe place.

"I don't hog the ER," Patsy said.

"Sorry, take it up with Dr. Armistead. He's the boss," Sammy told her with a shrug. "I gotta run. Dr. Armistead's in OR two and waiting for you."

With that the girl turned and power-walked down the hallway. She'd done her task and was now on to better things. Patsy felt a cold sweat break out on her skin at the thought of spending any time with Kyle. Besides the two incidences in the hallway, she'd done a damn fine job of avoiding the man for nearly a week.

But if he could be cold and professional, she assured herself she could be the same. That was her job, and she'd already decided not to let anything interfere with her work. She could act her age and behave like the doctor she was.

Stepping into the cold operating room, Patsy felt more than the chill of the temperature. She tried not to look to where Kyle was standing, but she couldn't help herself. He could've had her go to another surgeon, but he wasn't letting their lack of a relationship affect their working environment. He was obviously being more professional than she was.

But as her eyes made contact with his piercing brown gaze, she felt as if she'd been scorched to the soles of her feet. For the briefest of moments the look was so hot, so intent, so full of passion, she felt her knees grow weak.

Maybe he wasn't as unaffected as she'd assumed he was. Or maybe she was seeing what she wanted to see. Maybe she wanted him to feel something. If that helped her heal, helped her to move on, she'd take it.

Kyle kept the talk completely professional as the two of them performed a mastectomy together. It was a fairly simple surgery, but whenever they were dealing with a person's body, they needed to stay focused, especially when cancer was involved.

Patsy grew nervous as they neared the end of the surgery because the two of them hadn't been alone in over a week, and she wasn't sure if they'd step into the scrub room together, or if he'd try to talk to her.

She wasn't sure if she wanted that or not. She hated being unsure about anything. But as she finished the final sutures his pager went off, and he told her to finish up and then he left the room.

Patsy wasn't pleased to feel disappointment at his departure. She had to focus on her work. A month earlier that had been simple. Why was it that one person could affect another so much? Why did fate have to be so petty?

If she'd gone to another hospital, or Kyle had never returned home, she wouldn't be feeling this way now. So why couldn't she pretend there was no connection between the two of them and get on with her life?

If only human emotions weren't so damn overpowering. Wouldn't life be easier as a sociopath? It was a somewhat pleasant thought. It should scare her that she was wishing to feel nothing at all.

She finished her surgery, and her body hurt because she was so tired. She was on-call the rest of the night and couldn't leave the hospital. That made things worse. She cleaned up, called and checked on her dog, then stumbled toward one of the on-call rooms. Maybe she could grab a few hours sleep and save her sanity.

Instead, Patsy walked in with her head down, turned a corner, and ran straight into a brick wall—or what felt like one at least.

CHAPTER THIRTY

PATSY KNEW THE wall she'd run into wasn't a wall at all. She knew every inch of that hard body that had pressed against hers naked, damp, hard, and hot. She stumbled backward, hit something less hard behind her, and felt her feet twist.

Kyle reached out for her, making her flail her arms to keep him away. She had to look like a complete klutz, but she didn't care. All her thoughts were of getting away. She couldn't handle touching this man.

She went flying backward with too much momentum and felt as if everything was moving in slow motion as she crashed hard to the ground, her breath taken away as pain shot up her spinal cord. She couldn't keep the yelp from escaping as tears popped into her eyes.

Not again, dammit! This was how they'd met the first time, which wasn't how she wanted their last meeting to go.

She wasn't sure if it was because she was so tired, or if it was that she'd touched him, or if it was the utter humiliation of that moment. It all added up to a mess, and she wanted a Looney Toons moment of a black hole opening up and swallowing her whole.

But that didn't happen.

When the ringing in her ears lessened and the blurriness of her eyes disappeared, Patsy was very aware Kyle had knelt down in front of her, his face mere inches from her own. Her heart pounded as she attempted to scramble backward.

It seemed she wasn't in control of herself anymore, or her actions.

"Come on black hole," she muttered.

Kyle stopped what he'd been saying and looked at her as if she had a concussion. She didn't think she'd hit her head, but she could be wrong. Maybe it had happened so fast she hadn't noticed. Her whole body ached and was buzzing.

"Are you okay, Patsy? That was a hard fall." His words finally came through loud and clear.

"I'm fine. Go away," she said through clenched teeth.

She felt his hands on her, and everywhere he touched burned. She pushed at him, but he wasn't relenting.

"Dammit! Stop!" he thundered, surprising her. He rarely raised his voice. As a matter of fact, she couldn't remember it ever happening. "I'm trying to see if anything's broken." The tone changed by the end of his sentence.

"I'm fine. Please go away," she said, hating how close she was to falling completely apart.

"Not gonna happen," he said, his own voice irritated.

She glared at him before ripping her eyes away and glancing at the mess she'd made. She'd run into a medical cart and all sorts of supplies were scattered around her. She sat up and began gathering the items that would now have to be thrown away because of her clumsiness. No wonder medical costs were so high.

He didn't say anything as he started helping, picking things up and placing them on the cart. It didn't take long, and when they finished she had no choice but to stand. She was slightly frightened to do so, afraid she *had* injured herself.

It was slow going, and she pushed away his hand when he tried helping again, but she did manage to get to her feet, all while doing a mental assessment. She'd have a hell of a bruised tailbone, but nothing was broken—well, nothing except her pride.

"Thanks for the help," she said, not meeting his gaze. She turned to leave when he grabbed her elbow.

This time she managed to keep herself from ripping away from him and ending up in another heap on the floor. She'd have to get used to having his touch at times. They worked in tight spaces and that happened. It hadn't ever been a problem for her before, and she wasn't going to let it be a problem now.

"We need to talk," he told her. Finally she met his eyes and was confused with the anger and a tinge of concern in his expression. Those tears she tried so desperately to keep away were close to the surface.

"No, we don't. We're both professionals. We had a thing, it didn't work, now we need to work together without being teenagers about it," she said. That was the extent of the talk she was willing to have with him.

She was fascinated by the flare of rage flashing in his eyes before he managed to bank it down. The man had impressive self-control. She had to give him that. But it's also what made him so damn cold.

"I guess you did act like a teenager when you ran off, leaving me at a party we'd come to together," he said.

She glared at him, offended he dared to bring up the party after the humiliation he'd put her through there. She took in several deep breaths before she said anything to him.

"You were perfectly entertained at the party and I got tired of watching it," she said. She had to widen her eyes to keep the tears from coming. Damn him.

"What are you talking about?" The anger drained from his face, confusion taking its place.

"I heard you and Darcy," she told him. Her humiliation was now complete.

"What?" His genuine confusion confused her.

"I heard you and Darcy talking about all the surgery I needed." The last word was spoken barely above a whisper as those damn tears sprung to her eyes. She'd hate him forever if one dared to fall right then. She didn't want him to know what his words had done to her. She'd been humiliated enough.

His pager went off, and he glanced down and let out a sigh before looking at her again. He seemed to be searching for his own words, and she wondered what he was going to say to lessen what he'd already said and done. It didn't matter. He was probably looking to have one more night together. That's the kind of man he obviously was.

Before he could say anything, his pager beeped again and he swore, hitting a button before giving her his full attention.

"That's why you left? You saw me with Darcy?" he questioned. There was no expression on his face, so she had no idea what he was thinking.

"I saw *and* heard," she told him. "It's fine. You and I didn't commit to anything. We were having a good time. But I had no clue you thought there was so much wrong with me. I'd much rather sleep with a man who isn't so picky. Maybe I should stay away from plastic surgeons whose idea of perfection is ninety percent plastic," she said. Tears were choking her, but she held them back pretty dang well.

He suddenly reached out and grabbed her, surprising her too much to resist.

"Did you hear the whole conversation?" he questioned.

"I didn't need to. I heard enough."

His lips turned up, making her tears fade away to nothing as burning rage took their place. How dare he laugh at her when she was hurting so badly?

"We're fools," he told her as his beeper went off again. "Dammit! We'll finish this later." Without giving her a chance to do a single thing about it, he yanked her hard against him, his head lowering, and his lips taking hers in a kiss so hot she wasn't sure how they didn't melt together.

He pulled away, his eyes on fire, his lips turned up the slightest bit as if a weight had been lifted from his shoulders. She was completely lost. Without saying another word, he turned and walked away, leaving Patsy standing there unsure of what the heck had just happened.

Finally she stumbled into an on-call room, and pure exhaustion was the only blessing for her right then, because as soon as her head hit the pillow, she fell into a deep sleep, and nothing short of a tornado would wake her.

CHAPTER THIRTY-ONE

KYLE WAS CALLED into surgery all night, and by the time he went to seek Patsy out again, she was gone. There was no way he was hunting her down at home, not when he knew the kind of week she'd had. She needed rest.

He also knew he'd see her that night.

Stepping into his apartment, he moved to his counter and looked at the gold embossed invitation inviting him to Katherine Anderson's birthday party. He had to smile because he'd heard rumors of how Katherine's husband, Joseph, a giant of a man, liked to meddle in the lives of his family, and those he considered family.

And it was more than obvious Joseph Anderson loved Patsy. And that meant Kyle loved Joseph. Because after this day, after that kiss with Patsy, there was no longer any doubt how Kyle felt about her.

He had to do whatever it took to make her forgive him for what she'd misunderstood. If she'd waited long enough to hear the end of his conversation with Darcy, she would've heard him laugh at the vain girl, telling her that Patsy was perfection and someone who didn't need to change a dang thing about herself.

He shouldn't have stood there and played the game with Darcy, but he'd hated girls like her when he was a gangly, awkward teen with acne. He hadn't grown into his large frame and smooth complexion until he was out of high school, and girls like Darcy had made his existence a living hell.

His pleasure at taunting the snotty girl had ended though. He was done with feeling the need for revenge. He was at peace with himself. Maybe that had to do with Patsy. Maybe she'd change him in more ways than he'd imagined.

He'd been off balance from the moment he'd met Patsy Lander, and he had no doubt he was in love with her. Now he had to convince her that giving him her heart wouldn't destroy her life, they could have it all—career, kids, family. They could have the world if they simply opened their hearts to receive it.

The day dragged on until it was time for the party, and Kyle decided to have a driver take him. He wanted his hands free on the way home because he wanted them all over the woman he was going to take home and tie to his bed. From there on out he was going to ensure she didn't sneak off in the middle of the night again. He'd do whatever it took to keep her at his side.

If he needed to grovel, he'd do that as well. He was in love enough to realize his pride meant nothing if it caused him to lose the girl.

The Anderson mansion was unlike anything he'd ever seen before. Kyle had been surrounded by wealth his entire life, but there was wealth, and then there was *wealth*. From the second the car door was opened and he stepped onto the red carpet and walked up the giant staircase to the Anderson front door he was awed.

Music could be heard the moment he moved through the enormous hallways to the ballroom where hundreds of people milled about wearing red-carpet-worthy ball gowns and custom tuxedos that cost more than most people's mortgages.

The lighting was muted, and the scent of roses hung in the air as an orchestra played lively music at the right volume to allow conversations to continue for those talking, but an intimate moment on the dance floor for those who wanted to be in one another's arms.

Kyle searched the crowd for any sign of Patsy and was highly disappointed when he didn't spot her right away. He knew she'd be there. It was the only reason he'd decided to go. He'd find her, grab her, and force her to listen to him.

They'd already lost a week due to their stubbornness, and he didn't plan on losing a single minute more. He needed her, and he had no doubt she needed him just as much.

"You look pretty intense."

The deep baritone behind him made Kyle turn as he smiled at Ryan Titan, who had a stunning woman on his arm.

"You're gorgeous," Kyle said to Nicole who beamed at him. Patsy looked so similar to her, but the common thing that was most apparent was the kindness that shone from each of their eyes. That couldn't be bought, couldn't be surgically enhanced. True beauty lay in the eyes of a person, and Patsy and her sister shared the trait.

"Quit flirting with my wife," Ryan grumbled, but as he looked at the woman, the love shining in his eyes was apparent for all the world to see. He loved his woman getting a compliment that made her glow.

"Oh, you hush up," Nicole said as she stepped forward and kissed Kyle on the cheek. "If you're looking for my sister, she's over in that corner, fighting off a group of men."

Kyle's head whipped around as possessiveness surged through him. Before he could find her, Ryan's laughter pulled his attention back to the man.

"Wow, you have it bad," he said, patting Kyle's shoulder. "That's not easy for me to say as I've appointed myself Patsy's protector, but she loves you just as much. Stop fighting it and get yourself out of the misery you're in."

Kyle's self-control kept his jaw from dropping to the ground. That wasn't something he ever expected to hear from Ryan Titan. He might've expected to hear it from Nicole, but not her husband.

"Yeah, she does have it bad for you, but you hurt her at the party. It took a while for me to get it out of her, but flirting with Darcy was a stupid move," Nicole said.

"I didn't flirt with her. It was a misunderstanding. I don't like women like Darcy. I might've been humoring her just to be an ass," he admitted, feeling shame.

"What's going on with Darcy?" Ryan asked.

"She's a terrible person, Ryan. We don't tell you that because we love her brother," Nicole said. "I'll fill you in later." Ryan looked shocked. Kyle sort of liked how the man who had so much still looked at people through rose-colored glasses. It gave him hope for the human race.

"I do love Patsy. I screwed up pretty bad," he told Nicole. If her sister supported him, the chances of Patsy forgiving him leaned far more in his favor.

"Well then, you better go make it up to her," Nicole said. "And do it fast before Joseph gets a feather in his hat and matches her up with someone else."

He heard Nicole's laughter following him as he turned and moved through the ballroom. It was time to find his woman— and claim her. She wasn't going to be matched up with anyone other than him.

It was almost a Hollywood moment when the crowd parted and Kyle finally had his first glimpse of Patsy.

The sight of her literally took his breath away, and he stopped, rooted to the spot. She was a beautiful woman in every single way. No doubt about it. But tonight he saw her dressed to the nines for the first time ever, and damn . . . she was the most beautiful woman in the room.

She wore a long blue dress with a slit high on her thigh, the material molded to her luscious curves in a decadent way. The neckline was high, giving the appearance of modesty, but as she turned and laughed at something another man said to her, he had a jaw-dropping view of her naked back.

Part of him wanted to rush to her, throw her over his shoulder, and haul her into the first available closet. The other part wanted to drop to his knees and worship her. How could he have let her get away from him for an entire week? He truly was an idiot who didn't deserve her.

Finally he got his feet to move again, and their connection must've been strong enough that she felt him, because she suddenly turned her head and their eyes met, a clashing of lust, love, and a hunger so deep Kyle didn't care who noticed. All he wanted to do was pull her into his arms.

Slowly her lips turned up, and Kyle gazed at her like a love-struck fool, his cheeks hurting from the smile overtaking his features. They were going to be okay. He knew it in his gut.

He moved across the room, feeling as if he were floating. It was time to get the girl.

CHAPTER THIRTY-TWO

PATSY DIDN'T HEAR the conversation around her. All the voices faded away as Kyle glided toward her, a look of hunger, wonder, and what appeared to be love shining brightly from his eyes.

She was scared to hope she was seeing what she thought she was seeing. She had plans, dreams, lists to complete. She wasn't ready to fall in love. She almost laughed at herself as she had that thought.

It appeared as if a person didn't get to choose their own timeline. If she was in love, she was in love. There wasn't a dang thing she'd be able to do about it. And with the way Kyle looked at her, she didn't care anymore.

He'd wanted to talk. She was ready to listen.

Nothing in the past week mattered as much as how she craved to be in that man's arms. Maybe he was a playboy, but apparently her heart didn't care. Maybe she would end up a mass on the ground. But right now that didn't even matter.

He reached her and Patsy's heart fluttered. The way he looked at her took her breath away. Yes, she'd flirted before, but this was different. The intensity in his eyes made her feel possessed, made her feel she was the only woman in the world.

"Hi," he said, his lips turning up so much his beautiful dimples bored into his cheeks.

"Hi," she replied back, her voice husky and weak.

He laughed before reaching forward and tugging her into his arms, lifting her from the ground and spinning her in a circle. She joined him in laughter, feeling so much lighter than she had ever felt in her life.

"I'm sorry," he told her. "I'm so sorry for not fighting for you, for not trying to get to the bottom of things."

He set her down and cupped her cheek as he looked into her eyes.

"Darcy's hard to resist," she said, trying to mask the hurt she felt at saying those words. He obviously wanted her right then, and that's what she wanted to focus on.

Kyle laughed again and this time she wasn't amused. He stopped instantly when he saw he'd upset her.

"Darcy is a spoiled little brat who wants to get her way. If you hadn't run off you would've seen and heard that I was being an ass getting a little high school revenge on one of the popular girls. I can't stand women like Darcy, who think they need nothing more than their looks to get by in life. She was cutting you down and when she was finished I said that to her. It was petty and stupid, and had I known you were there I never would've played that game."

He seemed to be telling her the truth, and he also seemed genuinely sorry for his behavior. Patsy was amazed he had ever felt insecure.

"You had a hard time in high school?" she asked, more shocked by that than anything else.

"I was awkward, gangly and pimply. I hated high school," he told her with a shrug.

"Well damn, you grew into yourself," she said with a flutter.

Kyle laughed again while he leaned forward. The sound stopped as he took her lips in his, giving her a soul-stealing kiss that had her wanting to find a private room for the two of them really fast.

"I love you, Patsy," he said, blurting out the words as if it took a lot of effort to say them. She didn't try to hold back the overflowing tears at his admission. Before she could reply, he continued.

"I've never said that to another woman, not once. I wasn't looking for love, but damn it, I love you. I love your kind heart, your open face, your ambition, motivation, determination." He paused and wiggled his eyebrows. "I love your body, the way your curves fit perfectly in my hands, the way you moan when I run my tongue along—"

She laughed as she slapped her hand over his mouth and looked around, her cheeks flushed bright red.

"You can tell me all about that later . . . in private," she said, feeling so much joy radiating from her she wasn't sure she'd be able to contain it. "I love you too. I didn't want to; I wasn't looking for it, but I want to be with you all the time. I miss you when you aren't there, and it scares me. But I'm not ready to change my life plans."

She held her breath waiting to see if that wouldn't be enough for him.

"Then let's take some time to get ready," he suggested. "But right now I want to hold you tight on that dance floor, then I want to take you home, strip off that incredible gown, and kiss and lick my way along every inch of your silky skin. Then I want to hold you all night without you sneaking off." His words grew huskier the longer he spoke.

She sighed as she swayed against him.

"That sounds like my kind of heaven," she said.

And they did just that. He pulled her onto the dance floor and they ignored anyone who tried to interrupt them as they enjoyed being in one another's arms again. A week might not be a long time, but it seemed like forever when you believed the person you loved didn't love you back.

Patsy rode home with him, drugged by his intoxicating kisses by the time they arrived at his apartment. They made love until dawn broke over the horizon, then Patsy slept in his arms.

And it was right where she needed to be.

And she had no more desire to run anywhere unless it was straight to him.

EPILOGUE

SIRENS SOUNDED AS Patsy froze in the busy ER lobby, wondering what in the heck was going on. There were too many flashing lights outside the glass doors and windows for it to be a single ambulance.

She looked at her pager, and nothing was on it. She'd been paged to the ER, but the message hadn't been urgent so she was confused at the utter chaos that seemed to be happening.

"Come quick," Kian Forbes said as he rushed up from behind and took her arm.

"What's happening?" she asked, her heart pounding as she tried to assess the situation.

Kian didn't answer as he pulled her outside. She stopped and looked around. There were six ambulances, at least a dozen cop cars and several fire trucks filling the parking lot in a huge circle. All of their lights were flashing.

But nothing else was happening.

No one was running to the vehicles. No one seemed panicked. No one seemed to know what they were doing. This was what happened when there was a slow week at work, she decided.

Kian stood next to her as hospital staff members piled outside the ER lobby. The people who'd been waiting in the lobby, those who weren't sick, also piled out the doors, everyone looking at the slew of vehicles that were obviously out of place. She wasn't the only one wondering what in the world had happened.

"Dr. Patsy Lander report to the middle of the vehicles please." The voice came over a loudspeaker from one of the emergency vehicles.

Patsy looked at Kian who grinned and shrugged.

Roxy Forbes jogged up to them and grinned at Patsy too, as she placed her arm in her husband's. "I almost missed it," she said.

"Missed what?" Patsy asked.

Both of them shrugged. Pasty looked over and saw Nicole and Ryan with their three children sitting on top of one of the fire trucks. What the heck? She moved to the center of the emergency vehicles as people piled out of them . . . and music began to play. Her steps faltered and tears popped into her eyes as a couple dozen uniformed men and women began dancing to the tune of the music.

The song was *I Do Cherish You* by 98 Degrees. The sea of people dancing came closer and each dropped a few roses at her feet, and when the crowd parted there was Kyle, looking devastatingly handsome in a tuxedo with a microphone in his hand. He had one heck of a beautiful voice that shocked her.

He sang the chorus to her as he moved closer, then handed the microphone away as he dropped to one knee in front of her. Patsy barely saw through the tears in her eyes.

They'd been together for nearly a year, and once she'd let go of her fears, it had been pure magic. She hadn't lost herself in him. She hadn't lost her career. Her life had grown better because she'd let this man into her life.

"I love you more each and every day, Patsy. I wanted to propose to you from the moment I realized how much I was in love with you, but I didn't want to scare you," he said with a smile. "But I can't imagine living my life without you, so I asked some friends to come along and help me impress you."

"Oh, Kyle, I can't believe you did this," she said through her tears.

"There's nothing I won't do for you, nothing at all. Please put me out of my misery and tell me you'll be my wife," he said.

She laughed, a watery sound. She tried to speak, but it took several times before the words would form.

"I didn't think I was ready for love. I *wasn't* ready," she admitted. "But there you were, not letting me run away, not letting me betray myself. And now I can't imagine my life without you, either. I realize being a wife doesn't mean losing myself."

"Is that a yes?" he asked. He had a suspicious sparkle in his own eyes that she only saw when he was dealing with a child patient.

She was about to say yes when she realized his hand was empty. She smiled as she attempted a glare. "You're proposing to me without a ring?" she asked.

She heard laughter behind her. Then a few catcalls from some of the men who'd been dancing almost ballerina style at Kyle's choice of song. The men must've loved that one.

"Say yes, and you'll find out," he suggested.

"I should look at the ring first," she told him. They grinned at each other. "But I don't want to give you a chance to change your mind," she quickly added. "Yes, yes, yes. I can't wait to be your wife."

A cheer went up from the rapidly growing crowd of people. Then Kyle whistled and Patsy turned as someone released Eeyore, who ran straight at them.

Patsy laughed with pure joy when Eeyore dropped the same Frisbee at their feet that he'd jumped over Kyle's back to get that first day they'd met. Attached to the Frisbee was a box. Kyle pulled the tape off and opened it.

Inside were two rings, a stunning, indecently large diamond solitaire and a thin gold band, woven with tiny diamonds. He placed the large diamond on her finger first and it felt heavy, but it also felt right.

Then he pulled out the other ring and gave it to her. "I want everyone at work to know you're married, so I bought you a safe work one too," he told her. "I had it specially made to withstand anything."

She studied it, and it was made of a soft material that was flexible, but somehow they'd managed to get small diamonds into it. On the inside of the band the word "forever" was engraved.

"Perfect. They are both perfect," she told him. "Just as you are."

She dropped to her knees and finally kissed Kyle, which warranted another cheer from the crowd. They were interrupted by a happy dog as Eeyore's tongue swiped across both their cheeks.

"I love you, Kyle Armistead," she said as they broke apart.

"I'll love you forever," he replied.

Patsy hadn't known she wanted a happily ever after, but fate didn't care. It had given her exactly what she'd needed, even when she hadn't know she had. And she knew their love would be one that would last through time and all eternity.

Continue reading for an excerpt from the first book in this series. The excerpt is from **The Tycoon's Revenge**.

Excerpt from:

The Tycoons Revenge (Baby for the Billionaire, Book One)

PROLOGUE

A STAR FELL FROM the heavens and Jasmine watched in awe as the light slowly dimmed, and then disappeared entirely.

The feel of Derek's hand stroking her back was pure bliss, and she felt as if she could lie here all night long, never return to the real world. This place they'd created together was perfect — no father telling her it was wrong, no worries, no troubles.

"I love you so much, Jasmine," Derek whispered in her ear. "You are my world, my life."

"You know how much I love you," she replied, lifting her head to accept the gentle kiss from his lips. Her body melted all over again at his slightest touch.

"I hate having to take you back home tonight," he said, pulling her even closer.

"Then don't," she begged.

"Your father would hunt us down," he told her.

"I don't care. I know what I want and that's to be with you, Derek."

"Then we should run away together. I've actually been thinking about it a lot, about moving on from here." As she flinched, he added, "Only with you, my love; I'd never leave you behind.

Here's my idea. My dad will be fine. He's starting his new business. It's foolproof. He wants me to run it with him, but I have bigger dreams than running a computer store. I want to go to the city, intern for someone like Bill Gates, learn from them, and make something of myself," he said, passion flowing through his young voice.

"You already are someone special, Derek. You won my heart, and I've given it to you for life," she said, kissing his neck as the full moon washed its light over their naked bodies.

"You make me feel special — make me feel as if there's nothing I can't do."

"That's because you're Superman," she told him with a giggle. "Definitely more powerful than a locomotive…"

He laughed, then grew serious again. "What do you say? I'll take care of you if you come with me. We can get married and start our lives in the city," he promised. "You can even go to cooking school and open that café you've always talked about." He grew more excited as he spoke.

Jasmine paused as she thought about what he was asking of her. Could she leave it all behind? If Derek left, though, what would she have to stay for? Nothing worth keeping. She loved her father, but he was so cold most of the time — how much would he miss her, really? He'd eventually get over his anger and their relationship would heal, though it might take a few years.

Derek would have to come back. His father and cousins were here, and they were all closer than most families. The three boys were more siblings than cousins. She'd just be starting a new adventure with the boy she loved, but she wouldn't be cutting her ties here completely.

"Yes. I'll come with you. You have to give me a few days, though," she asked.

Derek pulled her on top of him with a laugh. Jasmine was a little sore, but the pleasure far outweighed the discomfort. The two of them made love beneath the stars, their joy shining even brighter.

They were going to forge a new path for just the two of them. Nothing could keep them from their destiny.

CHAPTER ONE

Ten Years Later

A NOTHER NIGHT, ANOTHER party, though for once probably not another woman. Derek Titan looked around the crowded room and forced himself not to yawn. He couldn't stand attending events where everyone drank too much, laughed too loud and tried far too hard to impress one another.

Derek knew he was what women considered a real catch. Hell, an idiotic magazine had published a write-up on Seattle's most eligible bachelors and ranked him, with his picture, as number one. He'd been furious and had tried to have himself taken out of the article, but his attorney had spouted some crap about freedom of speech. OK, so there were good points in the First Amendment, but he hadn't seen many. Since the article appeared, even more women with their eyes on a prize had approached him.

The magazine listed his net worth as equal to Bill Gates'. Though slightly exaggerated, that part at least was related to business. But of what possible interest or relevance was the hackneyed phrase "tall, dark and handsome"? So what if he stood over six feet and had broad shoulders? He gagged when he read of "rippling muscles." The flipping author even gave advice on how to meet him: don't bother with stalking him at the gym — he hated those places — but take up running, because he ran every morning, and sometimes in the evenings too, as a way to relieve stress.

Though it hinted, at least the article didn't quite say what happened after his second-best way to relieve stress. But here it was — the minute he'd finished taking a woman to bed, he just walked away, and that wasn't something to inspire the magazine's female readership. Sure, a lot of his women tried to get him to stay, but no one held his interest longer than it took him to zip up his pants.

He'd let a woman beat him once at the mating game. And after Jasmine shattered his heart and destroyed his father's business venture, he'd lost interest in the female sex — except, of course, for the sex. His priority had long been revenge. He figured that once he got it, he'd think about settling down.

A woman breezed by him wearing entirely too much perfume, and he snapped back to reality. He sighed, then grabbed a glass of wine from a passing waiter.

These parties were all about who had the most to offer. The women were on the prowl, and the men were fishing. He just wasn't interested.

He watched as a couple of superficial wannabe socialites passed by in low-cut gowns, dripping with diamonds. They were trying to catch his eye, and normally he'd make their day by flirting a little, giving them the impression they stood a chance. Today wasn't that day. He had a raging headache, and he was pissed that he'd been summoned to this snooze-fest.

"There you are, boy. What are you doing hiding in the corner?" Daniel Titan, his father, had walked up to give him the third degree.

"I'm wondering why I'm here when I'd rather be home with a scotch and my feet up," Derek replied.

"You're here because you received a request from your father. I have some things to discuss with you later," Daniel said in his no-nonsense voice.

"And it couldn't wait?" Derek questioned.

"Oh, live a little. You're always so busy adding megabucks to your bank account that you don't stop to smell the cabernet sauvignon," his father said.

"I live it up plenty. Hell, I was in Milan last week."

"You were in Milan on business. That doesn't count," his dad told him.

"For me, the ideal time is mixing business with pleasure," Derek said with a waggle of his eyebrows. Both men relaxed. "Seriously, Dad, I do have a headache. What's so important it couldn't wait until tomorrow morning?"

Once Derek had made his first million, he'd moved his father to the city. Daniel, now the chief financial officer of his huge corporation, had been instrumental in the company's swift and exponential growth. But his dad had gone through hard times more than once while Derek was growing up.

"David Freeman's here tonight, and he's talking to some people, trying to get new investors," Daniel said, his eyes narrowing slightly as he looked at the man who'd destroyed his livelihood some years before.

Derek was on instant alert. He searched the room, spotting his enemy. David was the one who'd made Derek the cutthroat businessman he was. "It's far too late for him. By tomorrow morning, he'll know that his company is mine, no matter what he tries tonight," Derek said.

Derek saw a beautiful woman approach David, stepping up on her tiptoes to kiss him on the cheek. David didn't even bother to turn and acknowledge her. The man noticed nothing around him if it didn't have dollar signs on it, not even his stunning daughter.

Derek's eyes narrowed to slits. He hadn't seen Jasmine for ten years, and those years had been very good to her. It wasn't at all what he'd been expecting, although, with her supreme shallowness, he should have known she'd have focused first and foremost on her appearance.

The top of her dress hugged her body, dipping low in both the front and back. Her curves were even more pronounced now that her body had matured. Her gleaming dark hair was swept up in a classic bun, with tendrils floating around her delicate face. Her chocolate eyes had once mesmerized him. They had a hypnotic quality, with a deceptive innocence shining through the thick lashes.

His gut tightened at just the sight of her, and that outraged him. Was he still a complete fool about her? She'd nearly destroyed his entire family, and yet he still wanted her. But that was all right. After all, his full revenge included her; he would have her in his bed again, and then she'd be begging him not to leave. Shrinks might call it closure. To him, everything was far more primitive.

"I'm leaving now, Dad. There's nothing he can do tonight, and tomorrow's a busy day for me," Derek said. After clasping his father's hand, he turned away and walked from the room without once looking back.

CHAPTER TWO

JASMINE SPOTTED DEREK across the room, and fire and ice waged war within her. How dare he walk around as if he owned the place? She knew the kinder, gentler side of him, but that boy was long gone. He probably never really existed beyond her girlish imagination.

The man she'd spotted tonight wasn't the boy who had taken her virginity and promised her forever. She wished she could forget that summer so many years ago when she'd waited at the abandoned church all day, waited and waited, hoping something had happened to make him late. As the sun had faded from the sky, she'd finally had to admit he wasn't coming. It had all been lies.

Just as her father had said, Derek had told her all he needed to get her to have sex with him. Once he'd added her to his list of conquests, he'd been finished with her. The remembered pain was almost too much to bear, even ten years later.

She watched him turning and walking from the room. He was by far the sexiest man at the party, with his custom tuxedo and piercing blue eyes. Although he sat in an office all day, his body betrayed no hint of softness. Her heart fluttered as she dwelled again on those long summer nights of touching and tasting those hard muscles.

Derek disappeared around the corner just as he'd disappeared that summer ten years before. Back then, she'd believed in fairy tales and magic.

No more.

Jasmine had grown up very wealthy in a small town outside of Seattle, Washington. Her father owned a multimillion-dollar medical-equipment company, and she'd always had more than most people could ever hope for.

Her mother had died while giving birth to her, and her father never remarried. He dated a lot of women, but none of them really acknowledged her existence, so she didn't grow attached to any of them. Sometimes, Jasmine had thought it would be nice to have a woman help her pick out a dress or teach her how to do her hair. But the staff, at least, always spoiled her a bit, which she knew irritated her father.

She'd seen Derek in school from the time she was young, but she got to know him only the summer before her senior year in high school. His family was dirt poor, but he was always determined to make a success out of his life and turn things around. He ended up helping her with math, and soon they were fast friends. She'd loved his hunger and motivation and the way he never talked down about anyone. She thought he was every one of her fairy-tale heroes come to life.

Soon, she found she was spending every waking moment with him. When her father found out she was dating a boy from the poor side of town, he'd been furious and demanded that she end the relationship. It was the first time in her life her father told her she couldn't have something she wanted. It also was the first time she'd defied him.

She'd continued to see Derek behind her father's back. She loved that Derek seemed to like her for who she was and not for her money. He wouldn't let her spend money on him — ever. He worked hard for a construction company, which would frustrate her at times because she wanted him to be with her and not at a job. He'd laugh at her frustration, but he always made it up to her on the weekends.

"Jasmine?"

Jasmine turned to find that she'd completely tuned out of the conversation. Normally, she was the epitome of cool — making sure to schmooze with her father's investors. That was her job at these functions.

More than once she'd had to fend off the advances of some dirty old man. It was a source of contention between her father and her — just one of many.

She wouldn't sell her soul to the devil, even if the devil was dressed in a hand-tailored business suit. Money had its uses, and she certainly needed a lot more than she had, but she wasn't for sale, not at any price.

"I'm sorry. I have a slight headache tonight and it's made me lose focus," she answered sweetly to the sixty-year-old who was leering at her. She had to fight the shiver threatening to travel down her spine at the lust in his eyes.

"I was just telling your father that I would love to have the two of you up to my lake house sometime real soon."

No way in hell! That is what she wanted to say.

"That sounds like a very pleasant weekend. Make sure you have my father notify me of when," she answered instead, already planning a convenient illness.

The man beamed at her; his hand came up to rest on her upper arm, and then his finger trailed downward.

"Excuse me. I need some medicine for this annoying headache," she said, discreetly extracting herself from the man's slimy grip and walking away. She was on the verge of being sick. How many more of these functions would she have to attend before she'd had enough?

Seeing Derek tonight had been too much. Wasn't time supposed to heal all wounds? In her case, ten years obviously hadn't been enough time. Seeing her first love — the only man she'd ever loved — was just too much.

It was time to leave.

Tomorrow would be a better day. That had become her motto for the last decade. One of these days, maybe it would.

As she walked from the party, Jasmine thought back to the day that her innocence had been stolen from her, the day that she'd realized she couldn't trust her heart, and she certainly couldn't trust men…

CHAPTER THREE

ARRIVING HOME AFTER being out all night, Jasmine felt her knees shaking. As she stepped through the doorway, her father was standing there, his face blotched with color, and spittle flying from his lips.

"I love him, Dad," she said, firming her shoulders as she faced down the man who instilled the very meaning of the word fear inside her.

"You don't know what love is. You are only seventeen," he shouted, stepping closer.

For the first time, she feared he might strike her. He'd never been a caring or engaged parent, but he'd never physically abused her.

"We're going to get married." She knew she couldn't just run away now. If she wanted to be a grown-up, then she needed to make grown-up decisions.

For a moment, his face got even redder, and then his shoulders sagged as he looked at her, anger seeming to fade away as sorrow filled his features.

"Have I been that terrible a father?"

"No, it isn't that, Dad. It's just that Derek and I want to be together. His father is starting a new business, so Derek can leave feeling right about it, and he's going to the city to make something of himself. He will do it, too. He's smart and strong and brings me such joy," she said. Maybe her father would really listen to her for once.

Walking over to her, he leaned down and kissed her cheek. "When did you grow up?" he whispered, making her heart leap.

She had never thought he'd be so willing to accept her decision. She'd thought that she would be leaving the house with him hating her, that it would take years for them to reconcile. She loved Derek enough to risk that, but the thought still saddened her.

"I don't know. Being with Derek is just…just like bees and honey. We fit and he makes me feel grown." What better explanation was there?

"What is this business his father is attempting? Maybe I can help in some way."

In her excitement to earn her father's approval, she never once thought he could be up to no good. This was her dad — the man who had raised her.

"I'm not sure exactly. It's a computer store, I think."

"I will speak to the bank, make sure the loan goes through for his new business."

"You'll do that, Dad?" How could she ever have thought her father cold or uncaring?

"There isn't anything I won't do to make you happy, princess," he assured her.

They spoke long into the night. She told her father everything, how she and Derek would meet at the church — all of it. Her dad kissed her goodnight and she fell asleep while still planning the future.

That night she called Derek and told him she had a surprise for him, that he would find out at the church when they met. He tried to get her to talk about it, but her dad had told her it would be more meaningful if she did it in person on the day they started their new life.

Because she now had her dad's permission, she thought it a little silly to meet at the church instead of just having him pick her up, but in her romantic heart, it was what she wanted to do, and her father agreed. The church signified the start of a new life.

She anticipated the surprise on Derek's face, and the joy that would flow through him.

Two days later, Jasmine had her bags packed and went in to tell her father goodbye. He hadn't always been the best father, but he had still raised her all on his own, and her eyes filled with tears as she approached him.

"It's time, Dad," she whispered, amazed by how much it hurt to leave. The ecstasy of being with Derek forever outweighed the pain, though. And now there wouldn't be any estrangement; her father was supporting her all the way.

"I can't believe you are moving to the city. Just remember your promise. You won't get married without me there." David was all smiles as he spoke to his daughter.

"I am so happy you want to be there," she said, throwing her arms around his neck.

"I couldn't miss my baby girl's wedding. Before you go meet Derek, can you do me a favor first? I have an important package that needs to be signed for and I have to run to City Hall for a meeting. Would you wait for it before you go?"

Derek didn't have a cell phone, and she couldn't reach him at his house, but he would be fine if she ran a little late. He knew from experience that she wasn't always punctual, and he'd understand. This was a last request from her dad, and they were parting on good terms.

"Of course, Dad. When will the package arrive?"

"It shouldn't be more than an hour," he promised before kissing her cheek again and then heading out the door.

It was two hours. Jasmine rushed out the door, and made her way to the church fueled by excitement. She carried only a backpack and a small suitcase filled with items she'd need the most. Her father said he'd send the rest when they reached their destination. Fueled by young love and needing nothing more, she was off.

She couldn't believe how good her father was being about all of this.

Derek wasn't there when she arrived, but Jasmine wasn't worried. He'd probably gotten held up, just as she had. Sitting down on the broken church steps, she looked out at the surrounding woods, listening to the sounds of birds chirping, and squirrels scampering through the tree branches.

When an hour passed, she began to grow concerned. Derek was always on time, and this was a big day for the two of them. Wouldn't he send one of his cousins if he were going to be this late? She couldn't imagine that he'd have come and gone. He would have waited, knowing she had been held up since that had often happened while they were dating.

When the sun started to set, she didn't even notice the tears tracking down her face. Maybe he'd changed his mind. Why? What could have possibly made him do such a thing?

She finally accepted he wasn't coming and dragged herself home, crying the entire way. When she walked into the house and her father saw her, he took her into his arms, cradling her the way he'd done when she was a small child.

"What's wrong, Jasmine?" His voice was full of concern.

"He wasn't there. I don't understand," she said between sobs.

"Oh, sweetie, this is what I was worried about," he cooed, making her cry all that much harder.

When she couldn't cry anymore, she made her way to her room and lay alone on her bed, clutching the one picture she had of Derek and her to her heart. Something had to be wrong. He wouldn't have left her there without a valid reason.

Working up the courage to call, she sat with the phone in her hand for almost an hour. Finally, she dialed his house and sat there, holding her breath, as it rang on the other end.

"Hello?" It was Derek. He was home!

She began to smile. Something had come up. It wasn't that he'd left without her.

"Derek?" she barely whispered. Her throat was raw from all the tears she'd shed.

"I have nothing to say to you," he growled into the phone.

"I…I don't understand," she choked out. Never before had she heard him sound so cruel. His voice was nearly devoid of emotion, just an icy chill running through the line of the telephone.

"You and your father are scum. You'll one day reap what you sow."

The call disconnected and Jasmine stared at the phone for what must have been forever.

"Jasmine?" She looked up to find her dad in the doorway.

"I…What… He sounded so horrible," she said, looking at her dad for answers.

"You shouldn't have called. He made his decision when he left you waiting for him. I never trusted the boy. That's why I had wanted to keep you apart, and I shouldn't have relented, shouldn't have hoped that he was different. Boys like him want one thing, and once they get it, they throw the girls away like they are nothing more than trash. You are better off without him, Jasmine. You'll come to see that soon. We'll just move forward now."

Jasmine lay back down as her father shut the door. Maybe he was right. Maybe Derek had gotten all he'd wanted and he was now done. Sobbing until exhaustion pulled her under, Jasmine felt she'd lost her innocence that night. Her days of being a trusting teenage girl were gone forever.

CHAPTER FOUR

EREK SAT BACK at his desk, a Cheshire Cat grin dominating his face. The papers were all signed, and now he was the owner of Freeman Industries. He had taken it right out from under David without the bastard having any idea of what was going on. Bad management had left the stocks cheap and easy to buy up.

Though David knew his company was in trouble, the hostile takeover had to have blindsided him. Derek couldn't help but gloat that David had walked into his former offices today only to be met by Derek's security.

Oh, yes, Derek had been tempted to be there, to be sitting in the man's former chair, just to see his reaction. He'd barely been able to stop himself, but he had plenty of time to wallow in his victory. He turned around and stared out the huge windows of his office at Titan Industries, looking down at the thriving city of Seattle. Acquiring a new company always gave him a sense of pride, but this one was special. It was the pinnacle of everything he'd been working for over the past ten years.

Derek heard a commotion outside his office and turned around to find that the man in question had barged in through his doorway. Speak of the devil.

Derek's secretary came chasing after him. "Sir, you can't go in there," she was gasping out, her voice and eyes panicked.

"It's OK, Lana. I can handle this," he told her.

She apologized and stood there, not knowing what to do.

"You can call security. I have a feeling Mr. Freeman will need to be escorted from the building once we are done talking." The smile never left Derek's face. This confrontation was coming far sooner than he'd expected, and he was enjoying it thoroughly.

"You worthless piece of shit!" David yelled.

"It's good to see you again, David," Derek said, not losing an atom of his cool.

"I was getting things straightened out, and then you swoop in and steal my company out from under me," the man continued to yell.

He was so angry, his face had become completely red, and his voice shook, along with the rest of him. The angrier David got, the calmer Derek felt.

"I guess you should have run your business a bit more lawfully and not left it vulnerable to a takeover," Derek said.

David looked murderous, intent on strangling him if he could make a dash across the room. Derek looked him over with a satisfied contempt. When he was still a teenager, Jasmine's father had seemed larger than life, but he now looked shrunken and old before his time. No threat at all.

"I ran my business successfully for over forty years, you pompous piece of trash. You may have the rest of the world fooled, but I know where you come from, and I know who you really are," David spat.

Finally, small cracks appeared in Derek's calm. He narrowed his eyes. But he refused to give the man who'd changed his life ten years earlier the reaction he was obviously angling for.

"Unlike you, David, I kept a watchful eye over my business. I may have grown up on the wrong side of town, as you've always liked to point out, but I made choices to change my life. I started with nothing; you're the one who will end up with nothing." Derek's smile mocked the adversary he'd thoroughly bested.

David lunged at him just as the security guards entered the room. Derek held his hand up to stop them from grabbing the man. He wanted David to try to throw a punch. Derek was normally not a violent man, but it would be a total joy to knock David across his pathetic jaw.

David saw the look in Derek's eyes and quickly backed down. "This isn't the last you'll hear from me."

"Security, please escort Mr. Freeman from my building. Let the front desk know he's no longer welcome on the premises." Derek then turned his back on him.

"I'll get you for this; just you wait," David shouted as he was dragged away.

Derek sat down and once again looked over the papers that gave him ownership over Freeman Corporation, with a satisfied smile. He pressed his buzzer. "Lana, would you please pull up those financial documents?"

She brought the material to him, and he got to work. He hadn't done his usual homework when acquiring the corporation. Before he took a business over, he normally knew it inside and out. He simply hadn't cared with this one — he was buying it up no matter what lay beneath the surface. He didn't even care if the buy ended up costing him millions. He had money to spare. This was about his pride, and nothing more. This was payback.

As he studied the papers over the afternoon, he was surprised to find there were some legitimate reasons to keep the company as it was instead of splitting it up and selling it off, as he'd expected to do. If David had run things the way he should have, the corporation would never have been in jeopardy of a takeover. The man was more of an idiot than Derek had originally thought.

He'd have to think about what he was going to do with this one. If he decided to leave it intact, the first thing to go would be the name. Derek refused to leave that miserable man's name attached to any aspect of the business. If he kept it, it would become Titan Medical.

The corporation was a major producer of medical equipment. The product was of high quality, but the marketing department was an abject failure. If the right people were brought in, the company might be worth keeping together.

As he studied through the financial files over the next several days, he discovered that David had apparently embezzled millions of dollars — another of the reasons the company was in such a weak state. He'd leave the legal department to look further into it. No, he wouldn't mind one bit if the man ended up in prison. It would just be icing on the cake.

The minute David had the corporation go public, he had investors to be accountable to. Since David had been stealing from those investors for years, they were going to want answers. Derek's smile grew even wider as he thought about David's life continuing to go down the drain. No, he hadn't always been such a brutal businessman, and he should have felt some shame now at his unholy delight. But he didn't, not in this moment of triumph.

David and Jasmine had ruined his father's chances of getting his own life back on track. They'd stolen his business from him, and they'd be victims of payback for some time to come. They were definitely reaping what they'd sowed so many years earlier.

He decided to keep the current staff for now, but he had memos sent out notifying them that they were going to have to defend their jobs. He normally left all of that for his staff to sort through, but since he was taking this operation personally, he'd decided to conduct a number of the interviews himself.

As Derek prepared to head to the former Freeman Corporation offices with a couple of trusted associates, he was filled with pride. Although he'd made the decision to keep the company essentially as it was, there would be a lot of people losing their jobs and a lot of new hires. It would take months to get everything straightened out.

Time made no difference to him.

As he walked from his office to catch the elevators, his dad approached. "Where are you off to, son?"

"I'm going over to the new company today. I have to eliminate some staff and get the HR set up to hire new employees," Derek said.

"I'll come with you." Daniel climbed in the elevator with him.

"That would be great. I could use an extra person, one I trust, and you're an excellent judge of character," Derek told his dad. He knew his father had a soft heart, but he was also a shrewd businessman.

"Son, I know this has been your dream since that low-life dirt-bag hurt you, hurt all of us, but you need to remember that most of these employees didn't even know David Freeman. They're just like you and me, trying to make a living," his father said.

"I hate it when you're right, but I know. Most of the people in executive positions will be replaced, of course. I simply can't trust anyone who worked closely with David. I'm not worried about any of the factory workers. My staff will make sure all of their background checks pass muster, but other than that, I'll leave them alone — well, not entirely," he added.

"What do you mean?" his dad asked.

"David was underpaying the factory workers while padding the executives' pockets. They are barely making minimum wage." Derek almost sputtered. "I'm going to raise their pay and offer bonuses for high work production and early completion of projects."

"That's why you're so successful, son. You actually care about the core of the company," his father told him.

Derek knew what it was like barely to be able to survive, and he followed the Golden Rule when it came to his employees. And so his turnover rate was low — once people came to work for him, they didn't leave.

"The bastard didn't even offer health insurance for his factory workers. It really is no wonder he lost everything," Derek continued to rage.

"Well, just remember that these people are scared about their jobs and don't know that you're different. It would be a good idea if the first thing you do is call a meeting and reassure them," Daniel said.

"You're right again, Dad. I wasn't planning on doing that personally, but I'll call a meeting first thing tomorrow. But, I want to spend today looking around and then eliminating some of the deadweight."

"Sounds like a plan, son." Daniel slapped Derek on the back.

A few days later, Derek rode to the new office building in silence. He was immensely satisfied to see the crew working on the new sign out front. Titan Medical was on its way up. He couldn't wait for it to be unveiled.

Derek walked into the building surrounded by his best team members and his father. He knew they made an intimidating sight, but he did his best to make eye contact and not frighten the regular staff. They were just trying to make a living, and none of them knew what David had been up to for years.

His team approached building security. That had been the first change he'd made. He always put in his own security team immediately.

"Good morning, Mr. Titan. It's good to see you," the guard said.

"Hello, Tim. How are things going here?"

"Everything has been mellow the last few days. Mr. Freeman tried to come in the day after the takeover, but he was escorted out and hasn't been back since," the man reported.

"I've had new badges created, and no one will enter without one after today. All employees who are kept on will receive a badge before they leave work. There will be a lot of people let go, and I don't need them sneaking back in and causing trouble. I also want several security personnel up on the twenty-fifth floor to escort people down as soon as they're let go. Today, unfortunately, isn't going to be a pleasant one."

"No problem, Mr. Titan. I'll send them up right away," he answered.

"Here's your new badge and some for your men. Crews will be here over the next few days setting up keypads for all the el-

EXCERPT FROM: THE TYCOON'S REVENGE

evators and exits. Here's the list of people who will be doing the work. These people, and only these people, are allowed in. If their company tries to send over replacements, call me and I'll let you know if they're approved or not," he finished.

"OK, boss," Tim replied, and then set to work making phone calls.

Derek spent the first part of the morning exploring the huge building in more detail than he'd managed to do the other day. Most of his time was spent down on the bottom floors, assessing the factory and its workers. They were eyeing him with trepidation, and he knew his father was right. He needed to speak with them soon. The work was going slowly, and he saw obvious mistakes being made. He knew that part of the reason had to do with their lack of enthusiasm for underpaid work, and part was because that they were so unsure of their futures.

He decided to call a meeting right away.

He spoke to his men, who went in search of the foreman or forewoman on each floor. In only half an hour, he had all the factory workers assembled. He looked out at about five hundred apprehensive faces. Even in Seattle, the job market for workers with their skills was in the dumps, and everyone was afraid of helping to swell the ranks of the unemployed.

He stood at the makeshift lectern and grabbed the microphone. "You all look worried, so I'll cut to the chase. My name is Derek Titan, and I'm the new owner of this corporation. First, I want to assure you all that we plan to keep this business up and running." He could hear a whooshing sound as many in the audience breathed out a sigh of relief.

"There will be some changes made, but I think you'll like what we have in mind. It will benefit every one of you. I've looked through the financial records, and you've been woefully underpaid and not offered any benefits. You'll receive a ten percent wage increase, and health insurance will be provided. By the end of the day, you'll receive paperwork showing the changes. You'll have to go through a background check to continue working here, but you'll see that the working environment is going to be much better from here on out."

He now saw smiles in front of him, and some mouths gaped open. He had to fight his own smile from spreading across his face. He needed to appear confident and in charge. He couldn't appear to be a friend — the boss had to be respected, not necessarily liked — but these people deserved a lot better than they'd had under David.

"If you work hard for me and meet production deadlines, you'll be rewarded. I want to turn this company around into what it should be. You make high-quality products here, so let's be a high-quality company as well. I want investors to walk through these stations and see happy employees doing a top-quality job. The better you do, the more bonuses you'll get. We'll be setting up some HR representatives down here and bringing each of you in over the next few days to sign paperwork. This is a new corporation, and if you do choose to leave, we'll offer you a severance package. If you have any questions, please wait until you're called in so we can move things along quickly Anyway, please return to work, and your bosses will be calling you in over the next few days. I need all the supervisors to meet me over here, please," he concluded.

He explained to the supervisors what they'd be doing in more detail, made sure the employees staying would be cleared for their new badges, and then made his way up to the executive offices for the first time since the takeover. A few secretaries glanced warily at him as he passed, but not many other people were around.

He walked up to David Freeman's old office and sighed. As he stepped through the doorway, he felt an overwhelming sense of accomplishment. The furniture had already been replaced. He hadn't wanted to sit in the same seat or use the same desk as that man. He hadn't touched the other offices, but this one would be his when he was working there, and it needed to suit him and the way he worked. And that wasn't at all the way David Freeman had worked.

He sat down in his chair and turned it toward the large windows. The space wasn't as nice as the one back at his main office, but it would do. There were brand-new cherry wood floors and comfortable but elegant furniture. Priceless pieces of art hung on the walls and a top-of-the-line computer system had been installed. He knew it showed weakness, but because of his beginnings in poverty, he liked surrounding himself with the finer things in life. And who would dare to say anything about it to him?

The view from the huge windows gave him a few minutes of peace before he had to continue his day. It was going to be a very long one, and he'd be lucky to get out of there before midnight. People were never happy to be fired, and he had a lot of people to let go.

He sighed as he turned back to the computer and started looking through the personnel files. It was time to learn who currently occupied the new offices at Titan Medical.

Printed in Great Britain
by Amazon

Printed in Great Britain
by Amazon

60288559R00132